From Tickfaw

to Shongaloo

From Tickfaw
to Shongaloo

by Dixon Hearne

Southeast Missouri State University Press | 2015

From Tickfaw to Shongaloo by Dixon Hearne

Copyright 2015: Dixon Hearne

Hardcover: 978-0-9903530-7-2
Softcover: 978-0-9903530-6-5

First published in 2015 by
Southeast Missouri State University Press
One University Plaza, MS 2650
Cape Girardeau, MO 63701
www6.semo.edu/universitypress

Cover Photography: Bradley Phillips
Cover Design: Carrie M. Walker

Library of Congress Cataloging-in-Publication Data

Hearne, Dixon.
 From Tickfaw to Shongaloo / by Dixon Hearne.
  pages ; cm
  ISBN 978-0-9903530-6-5 (pbk.) -- ISBN 978-0-9903530-7-2 (hardback)
  I. Title.
 PS3608.E263F76 2015
 813'.6--dc23
          2015006223

Dedicated to southern writer David Armand, without whose encouragement this book would remain a collection of bits and pieces relegated to the dark regions of a file cabinet.

It begins with a character, usually, and once he stands up on his feet and begins to move, all I can do is trot along behind him with a paper and pencil trying to keep up long enough to put down what he says and does.

—William Faulkner

If you want the unvarnished truth, they sent you to the right place. Come on in and sit down there in the parlor. I can tell you the whole damn thing: the fat little Catholic postmaster, the Bible thumper and the towhead, the cathouse, the popsicle woman, the postmaster lawsuit and kangaroo court, and Bert's 84-year-old mama doing a swan dive off a Gulfport pier—every bit of it.

Folks know I mind my own business and don't speak a word against nobody, but to tell you the truth, Bert Dilly is seven kinds of crazy. Did you ever see one of them little pug dogs? Ugly as can be till you get to know one personally. That's Bert Dilly up and down. Not one redeeming feature, and yet there's something kind of fascinating when you look him square in the face. Not ugly so much as odd. Goes right along with his personality. That man goes through life either excited or surprised. I can't tell the difference sometimes—he wakes up in a new world every day. Ain't got good sense on Monday, and come Tuesday morning, he can quote you the *King James Bible* chapter and verse. Got it from his daddy, Vesper Dilly, some folks say, but he ain't around to verify it. He died years ago when he got hit by a truck crossing the street downtown. Doctor said it broke every bone in his body. Knocked him fifty yards—somebody paced it off—and wrapped him around a pole right in front of the Two Moon Café. Not one drop of blood—but the look on that man's face still haunts some folks to this day.

Anyway, his mama, Lulu Dilly, is still alive and living at the rest home. Nearly dropped dead away herself when she picked up the paper one morning and found Bert's picture on the front page under the headline: "Postmaster Shipped Out Special D." Poor thing fell slap off her rocker and into a flower bed. Bert really takes after her side of the family, the Pitchers.

Old man Pitcher, Lulu's daddy, lived way out the Jonesboro Highway, damn near to Chatham. His family's been squatting on that land for four generations—won it in a poker game they say. But there's always been a dispute over it, whether or not his great-great-granddaddy won it by cheating. By the time anybody came forward with a formal complaint, the property had changed hands and the Pitchers had moved in lock, stock, and barrel—the whole clan. And wasn't a lawyer in the state who'd touch it, since gambling was as illegal as any other gentleman's agreement. I'm talking the very land Bert still owns out there—the last of the Pitcher clan with any legitimate claim to it.

But with so many Pitchers buried on that property, who in hell would want to fight him over a cemetery? They strew them bodies out all over the place, like they needed a lot of elbow room. Ain't none of them even got markers or headstones any-more. Back in the 1930s, one of the brothers got mad at the others and plowed up the property from fence to fencepost, and they lost all track of who and where everybody was laid to rest. Damnedest mess the parish ever heard of. And Bert stuck right in the middle of that one, too.

Bert's the kind that wouldn't deliberately hurt a cockroach, then turns right around and causes people misery. He's about your size, only rounder in the middle and walks pigeon-towed. No, I take that back. Bert Dilly ain't never *walked* nowhere—he's either trotting or galloping, that bushy shock of hair bounce-bounce-bouncing as he goes. Ain't got time to get it cut, he says, with all his work at the post office. And always humming. Lord, some-times I'd like to take a broom handle and knock his hummer into the next town. Miss Hannah—that's his sister—she got tired of it one time and stuck a hot pepper in his meatloaf sandwich and that shut him up for a pretty good while. You'd never know from that little packrat house of his, but he's a clean man.

Right out of high school, Bert's daddy asks him if he wants to go to college down in Baton Rouge, and he tells his daddy no.

And the very next day, he gets hisself a job at the packing plant with that K-Billy Bingham—his real name's Kingston Wilbert Bingham, so you can see why he shortened it. I tell you, them two should have been surgically separated back in grammar school. Bert can stay here, but I ain't got a Christian way to tell you where that damn K-Billy can go. You can't miss him, though—Bert, that is—him and that big-tooth smile and sky-blue eyes. Never cared a lick about anything but other people's business.

That's how the whole damn post office mess and lawsuits started. He does in fact seem to know everybody's business in town. Not that he would ever think about forcing open their mail, but he's found a fair amount of it poorly sealed through the years. And, of course, he took it upon hisself to personally inspect such items: love letters, divorce papers, deeds of trust, eviction notices, girlie magazines, Hollywood lingerie, men's trusses—whatever looked too good to just stick in a postal box or on the truck without a pinch or squeeze or a good shaking. And if the contents accidentally fell out—which they often did—he made sure they was secured when they left his counter. After all, he was the postmaster, he reminded folks, and responsible for every last piece of mail that shows up at his door—coming or going.

They would've reported him long ago, except that might perjure themselves for urging him on, asking who got what, who's doing what, and so on. Used to be, he just kept everybody up to date from postcards that came across his counter. But then it got much worse. Before long, he could tell you the contents of every last parcel that passed through the post office. Then somehow a regional postmaster got wind of the situation and came calling one day—without warning.

Soon as the Bunn sisters shuffle out the door, the man slaps a lock on it and posts an OUT TO LUNCH sign. We all know Bert Dilly brings his lunch to work every single day. Sits right there and eats it between inspecting parcels. That pitiful soul must've done some squirming and wiggling. Ten or twelve people pawed at the door and left their nose prints on the glass trying to see what was up. The only thing they could report, though, was a lot of finger-wagging and hand-wringing. And when the door finally pops open again an hour later, the visitor just smiles pleasantly at folks waiting at the door, positions his postmaster hat, and charges off down the block to his government car.

By this time, Nita Rae is back from lunch and wants to know what happened. There in the back room sits poor old Bert, white as a number 10 envelope, babbling and fanning hisself. When he's finally able to put two words together, he reaches out for Nita's arm and pulls her close. "I'm fired," is all he says. No need to ask why, she already knew. And though she never said a word, the whole town knew about it before closing time. We find out later that Crete Waller had dragged it out of that district postmaster down at Peabow's filling station; and everybody knows there's only one man in town snoopier than Bert, and that's Crete Waller. Shut off his pumps and called every last soul he knew with the news. Lord, folks was talking about it from Tickfaw to Shongaloo.

This might be a good place to tell you about how the Bible thumpers got mixed up in the middle of all this. I know for a fact they wish they'd minded their own damn business. But like every other do-gooder reformist, they thought the Good Lord must have sent them here for a purpose. Funniest-looking couple you ever saw, the so-called preacher a tall, gap-tooth, skinny man with crow-black hair parted in the middle. And with him is this squirrely little towheaded man in a yellow pinstripe suit. They just wandered onto Bert Dilly's property one morning and made camp.

The very next day, here comes the preacher and the towhead charging up Main Street like they was bringing news of the Second Coming. I almost crossed the street to avoid them. And Lordie, they have a mouthful to tell. Seems old Bert came out to greet them and they end up giving him the third degree. Yessir! Now you'd think the old fool would run them off with his shotgun, being so pushy and nosey. But, no! He escorts them right into his parlor and tells them the whole story—at least his version of it anyway. "Trumped up charges!" he tells them. "Harmless little thing," he says. And they believe every word, naturally. But what can you expect when you get three idiots together with only one brain between them.

So anyway, the two Bible thumpers take it to the street, and before the clock over at Homestead Savings strikes noon, that story has made its way from one end of town to the other. And it's damn surprising, let me tell you, to find out that Bert had been forced at gunpoint to open all them packages and letters under the direction of the Bunn sisters—please don't ask, it'd take too long to explain. Just know that their daddy owned most of this town at one time, and they think they still do. Folks just naturally hop when they say to.

Years ago, my Aunt Effie used to work out at the slaughter-house with Bert's mama. Back in the twenties, before she ever married and moved to town. Laziest man you ever saw, Uncle Tweet. Oh, that wasn't his real name, just something that stuck to him when somebody at the mill told the lazy lump he better learn to *tweet* for his pay. Bert's mama, Lulu, was kind of sweet on Uncle Tweet and found out he'd been courting Aunt Effie. There was a big ruckus one day, and Miss Lulu threw a rump roast at Aunt Effie and knocked her plumb cock-eyed. So Effie don't do nothing but lock Lulu in the cold storage closet for a couple of hours. And when they come and let her out, Effie tells them the door must have a faulty lock. Needless to say, that was the end of the little feud. Except that Bert's mama did everything she could to discourage him from courting me. She could have saved her breath and her blood pressure, too. I turned him down flat every time he asked me out. Let him court the old Bunn sisters, I said to myself.

Anyway, the Bible thumper and the towhead decide they've got work to do here, so they pitch camp at the edge of town and come trotting in every damn day to sell their Bibles and preach forgiveness and salvation on the street corner. Bert and K-Billy visit them out at their little camp site in the evenings, and before we know it they're thick as thieves. I guess old Bert thinks these two fools can pray him back into the post office.

I see we're both out of tea. Got a fresh pitcher out in the kitchen—I think better with a glass of tea in my hand. And mercy, there's so much tell.

So anyway, come Monday morning, in marches a fat little man with a black satchel and a clipboard—all business. Upset by the matter, Bert just piles in his pickup and heads off to his cousin's place over in Farley. The phone rings all night long—everybody knows everybody else's number for miles—so next morning here he comes rolling back into town again. It's the very first workday in anyone's memory that Bert ain't perched in his office among the parcels. Nita Rae is so tight-lipped on the matter, the town is ready to knock it out of her with a tire tool—good Christian or not. And the fat little replacement just smiles—rubbing his crucifix nervously—and tells everybody it's government business, and he don't know any more than that.

Of course, that's just a lie, and by afternoon somebody hits on the idea of getting together a petition to dynamite the fat little Catholic out of the post office and put Bert back in. And by five o'clock they have over two hundred signatures on a greasy, hand-written sheet of parchment—half the words misspelled.

The trouble is, nobody knows who to present it to. So, off they march to the mayor's house. Naturally, he's aware of the situation by now, but he takes grim exception to being dragged away from his summer garden to deal with a posse of gossips on the warpath. On the other hand, the election was only months away, and he'd already cut his margin close with the building bond last spring.

When the door pops opens, Mayor Purdy is met by fifty angry citizens, all talking and yelling at the same time. He slams the door in their faces, only to return seconds later with a bullhorn he uses to start races at the summer festival. He blasts the crowd with a lot of legal language, mostly about public disturbance, and when he finally has them backed off a bit, he proceeds to explain that the matter is out of his jurisdiction. *Federal* business, he says, and none of his—even if he did sympathize with the old fool. And then right in the middle of his apology, he steps back and, in a big dramatic gesture, points a stiff finger somewhere in the middle of the crowd.

"Shame-Shame-Shame on you, Faye Bawcom!" the mayor yells. "Shame on you, you Judas!" With that, the mob goes quiet and every eye turns toward poor old Faye. The shocked look on her face draws more than curiosity. She stands accused. Through his own nosiness, the mayor had managed to find out it was her that sent them letters to the district postmaster detailing every incident of mail tampering she'd ever been told about Bert Dilly. And now, here she is—the *hypocrite*—on the campaign trail to get the man's job back. Truth be known, she probably knows more about other folks' business than Bert and Crete put together.

Hemming and hawing, the pitiful thing tries explaining herself, that she never meant for it to go this far. She just wanted Bert to get a little reprimand for what he did to her. She'd been mad ever since he told Reverend Crowhill that she was exchanging letters with a man in Paris, France. Bert told the reverend that even though he couldn't read French, he could say with assurance that they weren't *church-related*. Even still, Faye knew a good thing when she had it—like everybody else in this town—and now she'd single-handedly cut them all off from their daily doses. We're not talking just a handful of busybodies with nothing better to do. Every doctor, lawyer, milkman, beautician, teacher, farmer, and waitress in town—small as it is—gets the *real* daily news from the post office. Somehow it seems to give the town a sense of importance all its own, someplace greater than itself. Where things happen.

Like the time Bert and K-Billy found that body floating face down out there in Bayou Desiard. Never did find out who the poor soul was, but not from around here—that much we knew for a fact. For all the attention it got, though, you'd have thought it was the mayor's wife. All them nosey people flocking over to Calhern's Funeral Parlor to gawk at the remains, like they knew her personally. The way they talked and carried on so, I tell you it made me sick at my stomach. The coroner said she was dead before she ever hit the water. Now how he knew that, I can't tell you. They rounded up every suspect they could find for three parishes and stretched that investigation out for six months.

Meanwhile, that body set over there at the funeral home—where they turned her into a popsicle—till they could sort the mess out. And every Saturday they'd wheel her out of the walk-in freezer for half an hour so folks could gawk some more. I tell you the whole damn thing sounded illegal to me, but the judge and the coroner both said it was alright, since the case was still open and somebody might come along and identify her. I don't mind telling you it gave me the willies just the same. What they did was put her in a casket with glass about two feet long on the lid. I was surprised how well it kept her all that time. Still I can't help wondering if she got freezer burn—being stored for so long. You know chicken and round steak don't keep more that a couple of months.

You can go out to Hasley Cemetery right now and see where they finally laid her away. And of course Bert and K-Billy volunteered to be pallbearers, seeing as how they're the ones that fished her body out of the bayou and knew her the longest. If you ask me, that was just another good example of Bert's little problem. I used to think it was because he read so many nosey detectives stories and fancied hisself kind of a private eye. That might just be at the very root of this post office business—like he was appointed by the FBI to check out every last piece of mail that came his way, looking for some kind of evidence. I guess you can see where that got him! Yes sir, I figured he'd be lucky if he didn't wind up face down in the bayou hisself and piled in next to the popsicle woman out there at Hasley.

So like I was saying, Bert no more than gets back from Farley to face the mess when Miss Nettie Moon sashays up the street to the courthouse, demanding they release every last record they had on the man. Of course they threw her out on her butt—her and her pearl-lace hat and ten-cent hairdo. But she wasn't through with them yet. No sir. She got her husband to call up the state postmaster office and tell them the whole story. Can you imagine what it must've cost old Joe Moon for that call? But the way I hear it, the old fool did all the talking on the phone—every word Nettie told him to say, that is—and didn't find out till later that the woman he was talking to didn't take down one single word because she didn't even work in that office. And don't you know Miss Nettie was fit to be tied when that bill came. I bet she's still over there trying to figure out some way to reverse the charges. That and filing papers for a sprained back she claims she got from the fall in front of the courthouse when they shoved her fat butt out the door.

You know, that same thing happened to me few years back when I was visiting my selfish sister over in Calhoun. I can see it plain as yesterday, her and that damn mealy-mouthed husband of hers setting there on the porch swing. And neither one of them gets up to help me when I hit the ground. The fall knocks me plumb near crazy, and there they set, gliding back and forth with their tea glasses saying, "I hope it didn't hurt, Raylene. Hope you're alright, Raylene." Like they'd give a good damn if I broke my neck. I was two weeks in a back brace I bought down at the corner drugstore. Couldn't bend over and touch my knees, and they wouldn't lift a hand to help me. Try taking a sponge bath for a couple of weeks where you can only reach your top half.

I think that fall was the very start of the rheumatism in my back. And that's how come I was right there the day they threw Nettie Moon out the courthouse door. I was coming out of the drugstore from picking up my back medicine. Lord, it was a sight, too, watching that woman trying to lift herself up all dainty like, especially since she's built for hauling.

The person I feel the most pity for in all this—except Bert, of course—is Aunt Flossie. She ain't really nobody's aunt—we all just call her that because we're so fond of her. You wouldn't believe it, but folks in this town are color blind. We don't care if somebody's purple, so long as they treat folks nice and don't cause trouble. You see, Aunt Flossie is a colored woman, but you can't get one person in this town to say a word about it. And she loves Bert like one of her own. She practically raised Bert and Hannah and J.T.

I remember it was a hot, sticky day—a pure-d scorcher—when Aunt Flossie comes trudging into the post office humming one of her favorite hymns. "Blessed Assurance," I believe it was, but she could sing it better than anybody. I know because she invited me out to Bethel Baptist, way out there in the woods—the only colored Baptist church around—and she nearly took the rooftop off with her high notes. Some folks still insist it's one of them snake-handling churches, but you couldn't prove it by me. Anyway, she's the sweetest soul you ever met. Everybody in town's heard her cut loose at least once. In fact, she used to sing on the radio every Sunday morning for a while over in Sibley, till they went broke and shut the station down. Lord, I love to spend an hour or two with her every Wednesday when she comes in for her mail. It's been her that keeps Bert apprised of what's going on out there in Pitcherville. She's lived right there all her life and witnessed three generations of Pitchers coming and going. She might be old, but her memory's like a steel trap. That's how come I believe her when she says to me: "There's something happening out there with Mr. J.T. and some beady-eyed man in a Cadillac." The man in the Cadillac kept pacing the property off, she says to me. You see, old man Greely, who she worked for twenty-five years, had left her a fair-sized plot of land that butts right up against the Pitcher property. Left it to her free and clear. Not that she needed it all by then, with all her eight kids grown and gone with the four winds. But it sure gives Bert a good feeling having her for a neighbor if he ever decides to rebuild out there.

The old family place went up in flames one night back during WWII when some of them kids was playing with firecrackers and set the place ablaze with a roman candle. Back then, the parish fire truck took about a week to get to a fire, and by then you've lost your ass and all the fixtures. Aunt Flossie says it was a sight though, with all them firecrackers flying all around the house. Lit up the night sky for miles, she says. That's when the last Pitcher,

Verna, moved into town and got religion. She met and married a man from church and he made a preacher late in life and they moved off to Winnsboro. A couple of years later, here she comes again, only this time prostrate and stiff with a yellow spray on her box. I guess she broke the Pitcher mold when she asked to be buried near her town friends out at Hasley. All the other sisters and their families made it clear that the land out there was hexed somehow, and they ain't been back.

You know, Aunt Flossie and Bert would make a good pair, the two of them out there together. She likes to know folk's business, too. Not in a pushy way, mind you, just a good listener. Everybody always felt like they could tell Aunt Flossie anything on their mind. And she ain't walked to town to fetch her mail in years. The minute she sets foot on the road, somebody whisks her up and brings her all the way or damn near it. I've seen Bert Dilly drive out that way deliberately to see if he could give her a lift. Right up to her old house—which has all but fell in on her a half-dozen times, and she still ain't got electricity. She keeps telling folks she enjoys the walk. "Refreshing," she says, but I know someday we're gonna find her out there stiff and baked by the roadside—laid flat by a car or sunstroke. Wouldn't surprise me if she ends up in the Pitcher resting grounds along with Bert and his mama's people. Since she got the news about the post office mess, she's looking forward to being hauled into court on Bert's behalf.

Anyway, it's a long time before townsfolk warm up to Miss Faye Bawcom again. What she does is she launches a little letter-writing campaign on her own—starting with the district postmaster. She tells the man she wants to withdraw her complaints and tells him it was just female problems that drove her to it. Then she dashes off a whiny telegram to the state postmaster, apologizing for the mess her report has caused and asks for Bert's job back. Even though not a word in her letter of complaint was untrue, she just couldn't stand the thought of losing all her friends and dodging hateful stares the rest of her natural life. She knew old Bert just couldn't help it.

To tell you the truth, the man sometimes reminds me of my cousin Les. A bona fide nut if there ever was one. Talks triple-talk and gibberish and never gets one damn thing straight in his life. Messes up everything said to him. *"Yeah-yeah-yeah,"* he says before everything. "Les, did you hear Burns and Allen on the radio last night?"

"Yeah-yeah-yeah," he says, *"Bert 'n Annie."*

Or "Les, did you read where President Truman marched with the Free Masons in New York?"

"Yeah-yeah-yeah. Night ridin' freeloaders," he says back to me.

I tell you, the man lives down the street from reality—somewhere in Bert's neighborhood. And though he scares hell out of citizens in this town, the kids treat him like one of them. I still remember the time he was hauled in for questioning when the motor cart plant went up in smoke. Happened right after his shift, you know. You'd think they'd have had better sense than let that man operate machinery to begin with, but they stuck him right up there on the assembly line. Actually, he was at the end of the line. His job was to take the finished motor cart and push it down the conveyer ramp.

Well, they figured he must have taken one of them motor carts for a little spin around the factory floor after everybody else was gone for the day and knocked a few wires loose, which set the place on fire. But they never could prove it, and he went right back to work on a judge's order quick as the plant reopened. And oh you should have heard them all telling about it. Before you knew it, they had Les convicted of drenching the place with kerosene and sticking a match to it. Worst lies you ever heard! But it backfired on every one of them, because they each had to take turns keeping an eye on the old fool till the day he retired. Old man Sumner, the boss man, said he wasn't about to get his butt in a legal sling with the government over some halfwit on the checkout line.

That was ten years ago, and people are still talking. Some folks just can't let go of a thing in this town. That's how come I know Bert Dilly ain't never gonna get clean of this mess. Lord, how people love to talk. You'll see what I mean when I get to the part about the trials. I did tell you there was two of them, didn't I? Oh, there's layers to this cake.

The first trial come about over the Pitcher land out there and Bert's handling of the family fortune—questionable as it was. J.T.—that's Bert's brother—he's the one that stirred things up. The man's ugly as homemade drawers and loony to boot. Just up and left here one day about ten years ago. We don't know what popped into his head, but the next thing we hear, he'd joined up with this traveling sideshow that blew through town one day. What they do is they put on little shows in the streets and parks—anyplace they don't get run off—and they eke out a living on the tips and donations they get. Of course they ain't rich, but they ain't any good either. J.T. always loved an audience though. I saw that show myself the very day he ran off with them, and we didn't hear from him again. Not directly anyway. They don't follow a straight route, just go wherever the wind blows them. But a year or so later, we did hear he was working the show with some chickens in a new act he cooked up, something about juggling live chickens to accordion music. Sawyer Teal seen him on his way to New Orleans one time, over in Natchez. Said J.T. had a big grin on his face the whole time he was throwing them chickens up in the air and catching them by the neck. And it made me wonder how many of them damn chickens ended up on the supper table, having their necks jerked so hard.

Like I said, we ain't heard from him for ten years—not until he blew back into town three months ago. You know, it ain't been easy on Bert's mama with so much going on around her, but I have to tell you she came from troubles herself, long before giving birth to her three kids. Her family—the Pitchers you remember—left her with nothing but a headache for an inheritance. Every last child in her generation is dead now, and there ain't one single Pitcher to carry on the family name. By law, that leaves Bert—being the eldest nephew in line—with the only legitimate claim to the Pitcher land out there.

From Tickfaw to Shongaloo

Anyway, like I was saying, Mr. J.T. suddenly comes blowing back into town one afternoon, acting like he's only been gone overnight. And when he finds out his daddy's died and his mama's damn near it, he decides that *he's* entitled to the family estate—even the Pitcher property out there. Soon as he hears Bert's up on a federal charge over the post office mess, he gets hisself a lawyer over in Hodge and files for a hearing, saying Bert ain't fit to handle the family finances and neither is his sister Hannah. Of course that money-chasing lawyer tells J.T. he can have the moon, and pretty soon, here he comes riding into town, passing out fancy cards right and left, trying to drum up even more business on the street. But little does he know how close the nuts fall to the tree in that family—Bert on his way to the Big House, his mama knocking on St. Peter's door, Miss Hannah ready for the playground, and his client J.T. a runaway from a seedy sideshow. No sir, he doesn't find out about that till much later. Naturally, most folks wouldn't give him the time of day, him being an outsider and suspicious acting.

So, now we got two legal investigations going on—three if you count the Pitcher cemetery mess—and Bert Dilly right there at the center like a bullseye. And what happens next is just too silly to believe, but here it is. You see, the whole time folks in town are letter-writing and phoning and telegramming Baton Rouge on Bert's behalf, J.T. comes right behind them phoning and telegramming whoever that law devil tells him to, trying to turn up the heat under Mr. Bert. Next thing we know, the law jackal gets on the phone hisself and calls up a law office over in Monroe and tells them he's got his hands on a bona fide felon up on charges of mail tampering, and he thinks there's land fraud and opportunity involved, and that this was too big for his little office over in Hodge, and do they want the case. And two days later, here he comes roaring back into town, a big city grin on his face and a briefcase full of papers.

Now what was in these papers was a matter of great speculation, because he was swinging it around everywhere he went. Wouldn't even let go of it to visit the privy, they say. But everybody knows he's just trying to make a big name for hisself at the sacrifice of one Bert Dilly. And it looks like things are headed south for Bert when he's handed the summons to appear in court for a hearing.

Looking back, I don't think Bert truly understood the list of charges against him, the charges that lawyer and J.T. put to paper, that is. The lawyer might have been out of his area with the post office business, but he could sure use it to tighten his case that Bert was unfit to handle family business. The post office charges was just the frosting on the cake. Oh, he's a slick one, that devil.

The night before the hearing I'd been listening to the radio and heard this man talking about the power of positive thinking—some loud-mouth know-it-all from New Orleans. Says all you got to do is close your eyes and pretend to be someplace else. Says you can will yourself out of any mood. And by the time I finish listening, I'm beginning to believe. So I says to myself, "Now you can do this," and I go to bed with a smile in my heart. And then I crawl out of bed and read the headlines next morning, and there's Bert Dilly's picture splattered like bird crap all over the front page, and I know right then it's gonna take a lot more than positive thinking to save his butt.

It's a hot day when the court date rolls around, and because it's just a hearing, there ain't supposed to be all these people there. But here they all are—the whole damn crazy bunch of them—all crowding in the courthouse like a pack of wolves ready to attack. Everybody and his grandma shows up wanting to know what's going on, and Judge Fryer just finally throws up his hands and lets them all pile in wherever they can sit or stand. And it should have been short and sweet, but it turns out to be one of the longest days of my life.

First, the judge asks the lawyer and J.T. to make a statement, give their reasons for the hearing. Lord, that statement goes on for twenty minutes by the courtroom clock, till finally Judge Fryer tells him to spit the rest of it out in a hurry, which he does.

It's a biography of Bert's whole life leading up to the recent loss
of his mind—every lame-brained thing he'd ever done, which
was ample, and how it has affected other people. He blames
Bert for making his mama crazy as him and why his sister Hannah is "a pitiful old maiden lady ashamed to bring a suitor into
her house—let alone her life." And there she sits, poor Hannah,
having to listen to these words right out loud in front of all her
friends and neighbors. So it's no surprise when she passes out cold
right there on the spot and has to be dragged by her arms into
Judge Fryer's chambers, where they stretch her on a cot and hose
her down with ice water. And let me tell you, that was NOT a
good thing to do to Miss Hannah. No sir! She come up off that
cot swinging and cussing, and the racket completely drowns out
the lawyer and the whole proceedings.

The judge bangs his gavel so hard the damn thing breaks
in half, and the head of it flies across the room and strikes the
lawyer in the head. And there sits the judge, sweating something
fierce and mad at everybody in his courtroom, all of us bent over
laughing at the lawyer man. We know we've gone too far when
Fryer takes off his shoe and starts pounding the bench with it. He
must have pounded for five full minutes, till he finally hikes up
his robe and stomps out the back, leaving the rest of us stuck for a
response. "Is he coming back?" someone asks the bailiff, and the
bailiff tells us we got five minutes to clear the courtroom.

Next morning the court clerk posts a notice on the courthouse door that ain't nobody but the persons on the posted list
supposed to be there when the hearing resumes on Thursday. But
let me tell you, that was still quite a list. The lawyer man wanted
everybody he talked to, to be there for the hearing in case there
was any questions. And there wasn't one single soul on that list
called by Bert in his defense. I think to myself, he's either a wise
fool or dumb as a stump, but I suspect a stump would have better
sense.

Like I said, the first day of the hearing was on a Tuesday. I
remember it clearly because that afternoon, here comes the *state
postmaster* gliding into town in his official navy blue Buick with

red and white accents, barking dust all over the place because
he took a wrong turn on the outskirts of town and wound up at
Eddie's Chicken Farm. So you know he ain't showing up with
a bouquet of hearts and flowers for anybody. He checks hisself
into the hotel right away—three doors down from the law devil.
Can you believe that? And folks just don't know what to make of
this—if the lawyer sent for him or just what—and he ain't talking. So we just have to wait it out.

In the meantime, the postmaster makes a little trip to the
post office and they tell me he had quite a long visit with Nita
Rae and reminded her this was official business and not to discuss
matters with another living soul. The only way we find that part
out is somebody overhears him reminding her as he's going out
the door. And you know that tight-lipped Nita Rae—I told you
about her earlier—she goes home and takes the phone off the
hook and won't talk to nobody. I suspect she's afraid they'll have
her up on some charge or other if she so much as hums. She's a
good Christian woman like I said, but you know how them others are—ready to beat it out of her like dirt from a rug. But she
don't budge, and you have to admire someone like that, standing
up to that ugly mob.

To this day, we don't know exactly what all that postmaster said to her. But you can be sure of one thing: he ain't got no
desire to come calling again anytime soon. Tate Foley seen to that
when he set off the new ceiling sprinklers over at the hotel in the
middle of the night, thinking the man would just pack up his
soaked clothes and head his car back to Baton Rouge. But that
don't happen. And that lawyer don't leave neither. In fact, what
happens is that Rona Meecham, the hotel operator, calls up her
friend Bonita McKay, who insists that the postmaster stay at her
house. Can you imagine the pump job he got that night? I know
he didn't get a wink of sleep. I heard that every time he looked
like he's gonna doze off, Bonita dropped her Bible on the floor.
And of course, none of this helps poor old Bert one bit. You know
how testy people can get when they ain't had enough sleep, and
that postmaster looks like a walking nightmare next day. Nobody
knows where the lawyer spent the night, and nobody cares.

Come Thursday morning, we all arrive at the courthouse bright and early—everybody except Mayor Purdy, that is. Seems quite a brouhaha had shaped up over in Hodge the day before, where the Mayor's Day Parade was going on. What happened was Clint Dody had driven his family over for the festivities. You know, a sort of getaway for the wife and kids. And halfway there his car took out. And there they were, him and Ethel and them five screaming Dody young'uns melting in the asphalt. That is, until along comes a laundry truck and Clint flags him down. The way I heard it was, Clint told him his wife was expecting again, and that's the only reason the laundry man even offered. So, they all pile in the back and off they go.

Now, by the time they make it to Hodge, them kids had turned that truck inside out, and the fresh laundry was tromped and scattered from dashboard to derriere. And all the commotion drove the laundry man to distraction, and he missed his turn and finds hisself right smack dab in the middle of the parade— wedged right between the marching band and the Badgerettes. But that ain't the half of it. Them kids just naturally think they're part of the parade, and they pile up in the cab area of the truck with the driver—two hanging out each window and one on the dashboard. The driver said later he didn't know which one took it into his head to take over the driving, but the next thing he knew the truck veered off to the right and SMASH—right into the pavilion where the mayor and city council and their wives are perched, and it knocks every last one of them off the stage and into the crowd. Worst traffic jam the town ever saw. The last one to hit the crowd gets bounced along over their heads like a water pail in a fire brigade and then dumped into Mayor Purdy's lap right there on the sidewalk—her legs over his shoulders.

Afterward, the town tries to sue the laundry company for all the damages, and them Dodys—if you can believe it—get off scot-free. And after that little episode, the laundry company added a back-up truck just in case—and a flat policy of no stopping en route. I heard it took them two solid weeks to sort out and launder all them clothes on the truck. That's how come Mayor Purdy is so late that morning of Bert's sanity hearing.

Anyway, sure enough, Sheriff Bates is there to shove people back out the door if their names ain't on the list—which the mayor's is. And there the rest all stand, fuming and spitting in the hot sun. And what I want to know is, with so many people off work, who's running the damn town? Half of them still think this is about that post office mess, even after Judge Fryer told them that this hearing doesn't have one damn thing to do with that. But you can't make people believe something they don't want to. Just like them Bunn sisters. Now, they were told directly that the hearing for the post office matter was a month away, but do you think that satisfies Tallulah and Opal Bunn? Hell no! They come stomping up the sidewalk, swinging their purses for people to make way for them. Suspicious! That's the whole thing: people are just too damn suspicious and nosey. I tell you this: what I know I see with my own eyes or somebody else tells me, because I sure don't go looking for it. No sir!

But there I am, right smack on the list—just because I happen to be Hannah Dilly's dearest friend. And her still puckered and sour over that "old maid" remark in front of everybody. Poor thing's gone through life apologizing for every one of them Dillys. And it just got worse after her mama came out of the hospital that time and Bert decided to take her on a nice trip down to Gulfport for a few day's rest. Just the two of them. Miss Hannah stays home where she can have some peace and quiet. But it don't work out that way. The first day they get there, Bert's mama wants to go straight out to the gulf. So Bert rolls her out on the fishing pier and parks her right at the end where she can have a nice view of everything.

Pretty soon, she decides she wants a cherry Coke and sends Bert trotting off to find her one. And when he gets back, she's gone. There sets the wheelchair—empty! Naturally, Bert starts yelling at the top of his lungs in all four directions, till somebody points him toward the water below. And lo and behold, there is Lulu Dilly, bobbing up and down with her slip up around her neck and gasping for life.

Well, in jumps Bert—right off the pier in his blue suit—and

nearly drowns them both, hauling her considerable bottom to shore. And would you believe not one single soul volunteers to help him land her?

So right back into the hospital she goes and stays there one solid week till her pride heals. She swears Bert to secrecy about her little stunt, but you can't keep a thing like that quiet. By the time they come rolling back into town, every neighbor on the block is there to greet them, toting covered dishes and get well cards. Everybody except Hannah. She took off to Jonesboro to escape the humiliation—her mama doing a swan dive off a pier into the Gulf of Mexico. Far as she was concerned, it just proves what everybody says about her mama—one deed shy of Cedarville. That's the state asylum, in case you don't know.

At least she'll have some company there. Her oldest friend Darla Birdlace is headed that way too. I have often suspected that every time Miss Darla stops to get air in her tires, she has them refill her head too. I saw her downtown last week gawking at something in a store window. I say hi to her—as is my custom when passing folks I know on the street—and she don't know me from Adam. Hems and haws, trying to think of my name, till I finally have to tell her. Even then she looks completely discombobulated. Like I gave her a trick question. I think to myself she must be getting senile—which nudges me a little closer to the head of the line.

Anyway, I says to her, "Darla, ain't you supposed to be over at the Beauty Barn? Never known you to miss your Thursday rinse."

"Oh am I?" she says to me. "Oh yes, that's where I was headed." Pitiful thing don't know if she's washing or hanging out, so I take her by the hand and point her in the right direction. And don't nobody see her for a week. The sheriff don't seem the least bit concerned though. Last time she disappeared, she got on a bus to Shreveport and spent three whole days in the bus station before somebody finally caught on that she was lost. And when they asked that silly bus driver that dropped her off in Shreveport, he told them she looked so pitiful he just thought she must have lost her ticket for the next connection to someplace. Well, she'd lost it alright—her ticket, her marbles, and her money, all at the same time. Somebody stole her purse and her new shoes, and let me tell you, it was quite a sight watching that woman step off that return bus with her feet coming slap through her hose. And why Shreveport popped into her head nobody could figure out. Ain't a living soul she knows there.

But enough about that, back to Bert's hearing. I must say the courtroom is sure toned down a bit when we reconvene. Right up front, Judge Fryer swears he'll hold every one of us in contempt if we so much as fart. Excuse my language, but that is exactly what he said—word-for-word! I don't use that type language myself, but if he can get away with it in a court of law, then I guess it ain't that big a deal. And then he tells us he'll stretch these proceedings out till Christmas Eve if he has to, because he intends to see that Bert Dilly gets a fair hearing. Well hell, you'd think he'd want to bring this sanity hearing to a fast close so we could move on to the bigger matter about the post office. I'm sure that's why that postmaster showed up for this silly sideshow, just so he can see for hisself what kind of people he's dealing with.

It seems that law office over in Monroe had authorized Mr. Lawyer Man here to negotiate a little deal with J.T. for the Pitcher property and get him to sign a partnership agreement to develop that land into good real estate. What J.T. don't know— because he never took a damn bit of interest in his family—is that the land has already been developed. Into a graveyard!

Can I get you another glass of tea? How about another teacake or two? I hate to keep asking, but it makes me nervous to see my company's tea glass getting low. My mama—rest her soul—kept a glass of tea going twenty-four hours a day, and everybody says I'm just like her. The tea, that is, nothing else. That woman was crazy as the day is long, bless her heart. Didn't know she was in the world the entire last year of her life. The doctor said one day she told him that Jesus was sitting in a chair out in the waiting room and he wants to know what time visiting hours are. And that had the doctor worried for a while—or scared—because he turned up the dosage on her IV and ran her blood sugar sky high and damn near had to call in the coroner before they leveled her off. So naturally the burden fell to me when they decided she might as well sit it out at home.

And of course my dear sisters—I told you about one of them already—didn't show up till the day we popped her into the ground. And that was just for appearances, just in case she had a few dollars holed away somewhere. They tore through that house like a pair of bush hogs, snatching and grabbing everything that wasn't bolted down, and then later found out that was all there was. Mama didn't have a nickel left in her purse—nothing but her lavaliere and wedding ring—which was to go to me or my other hateful sister Clareese, whoever married first—and her house, of course. But the bank owned that because we had to take loans on it to cover the hospital bills and all. So they haul off the best parts of Mama's life with them and leave me to mop up.

The very next night the plant burned down and threw me out of my job. I was at prayer meeting at my church, and here comes Bert busting through the door yelling at the top of his lungs, "Get out! Get out! The town's on fire!" And of course we all pour out the doors and windows—the closest hole we can find—and there at the other end of town the sky is lit up like the burning of Atlanta. Fire trucks come roaring in from Hodge and Jonesboro—any place they can find with a truck—but by the time they get here, the fire has jumped the road and set off the packing house too. And there's Bert and K-Billy at the head of the fire line trying to direct things: "You three go over there! Bring that hose over here! Turn up the pressure!" And they keep it up till a couple of the firemen chase the two of them off with a shovel and a pickaxe. So you can see how Bert just naturally insinuates hisself into everything. Lord, I hate to think what would've happened if they hadn't beat out the fire at the packing house. Nearly shut down the town as it was, almost a third of us out of work for six months.

That's how I ended up moving in with Uncle Fate and Miss

Clareese. And let me tell you, if that wasn't Hell then I don't know what is. Kind of reminds me of Bert and J.T.'s relationship, only the tension was a lot hotter in our hell hole. Sister-woman—that's what I call Clareese—flitting in and out all hours of the day and night, and then digging into Uncle Fate's bank accounts. Tells him I must've made a few mistakes in his deposits or in his checkbook when I went grocery shopping, and she don't know a thing about any missing money.

So I says to him, "She's lying," and he puckers right up with resentment. It's an awful sight, too, with only three teeth in his head. He was always partial to Clareese, her and her hateful, spiteful ways—wouldn't say, "Crap!" if she had a mouth full of it while he's around. Uncle Fate just dotes on her. And the poor fool wouldn't shake a finger at *her* if she set him on fire. So the next thing I know, he's trying to tell me I'm just jealous because Miss Priss got herself that job down at the bank and met her a man—and of course that's just another lie! We all know how she got that job, and it wasn't from clerical favors. Uncle Fate flinches at any suggestion his precious Clareese would do anything unclean, so I just go right on with my dinner.

Then before long, here comes Lady Astor herself, primped and powdered up so we nearly don't recognize her, and wearing mama's diamond lavaliere and gold bracelet. Mama left strict instructions that her lavaliere was not to leave her jewelry box until one of us married—and not a day before. But do you think Uncle Fate took notice of it? All he can say is what a fine figure of womanhood Clareese had made—"the spittin' image of your Aunt Lizzie," his late wife, he says. Made me so mad I could snatch her bald-headed. Sneaking into Mama's jewelry box against her last will. So then I says to her, I says, "Sister, ain't you ashamed of breaking your promise to Mama any such way, raiding her coffers before she's cold in the grave?"

"Hell no!" she says back to me. "Mama's gone now, and she meant for me to have them soon as I find me a man." Then she grabs a dining chair and cozies up next to Uncle Fate, winking and blinking and smiling the whole while. Me out in the kitchen,

bosom over the burners, and her upstairs plucking and painting a new face for herself. The thought of it just chapped my ass.
Then I says to her, "Sister, ain't you got altar duty at the church-
house tonight? I seen your name on the calendar last Sunday."
But I might as well have been talking to the pot roast for all the
response I get. She knows she signed up for it, but do you think
she cares? Next thing I know, she's got Uncle Fate asking me why
I don't go for her. This is where I draw the line.

"I ain't trotting off down to the church tonight, so you can
just forget it, sister-woman. You signed up, and you can just
march your prissy butt down there and break out the Brasso,"
I says. So she pouts her face up to hot pink and proceeds to tell
Uncle Fate how mean and hateful she thinks I am, and, of course,
he agrees with her. Reminds me of the time she signed herself
up for that magazine drive at school and told daddy it was all my
idea. And then the day before the drive was over—and she hadn't
knocked on a single door—she gets daddy to make me drum half
the neighborhood, and the next week she gets a Princess watch
for my sales. Daddy never could see through her neither.

At this point, Uncle Fate gets up from the table and hobbles
over to the window. "Look out yonder," he says. "That tree over
there. You see that tree? I planted that tree the day you was
born, Clareese. Ya Aunt Lizzie and me, we couldn't have any
young'uns. Never even had us a dog. That mimosa tree out there
is the only livin' thing we have to show for forty years together.
Or had—rest her soul."

A tear wells up in his eye, and I am truly moved by the
sentiment. But you can bet that Miss Priss would use it to her
advantage, and sure enough, she starts right in on Uncle Fate.
How important it is to carry on the family line. How she sees it
as her duty to find a good man to see that it happens. And how
that person might very well be the man she's seeing tonight.
How awful I am, not to do her church duty. And how bitter sad
it would be if she missed an opportunity because of me. All of
this conjured up right there on the spot—and Uncle Fate taken in
like a ten year old at a circus sideshow. The old fool! Then off she

traipses, leaving me stuck for a response. So I says to Uncle Fate, I says, "I ain't cloaking her sins this time. And when the sister deacons call here wanting to know where she is—and they will—you can just tell them she's out trawling for a husband."

The very next morning, in marches sister-woman, sits herself down at the breakfast table, and—not a ring on any finger—announces that she's getting married. Ain't known the man two weeks and she's ready to tie the knot. So I says to her, "Ain't that nice, sister. Where's the ring?" After a fair amount of hemming and hawing, she admits it was a split-second decision, and neither of them thought about it at the time, but they're gonna pick out something today. Naturally, Uncle Fate does back flips when she makes her announcement. Poor soul ain't got a lick of sense in such matters. Never occurs to him to ask anything about the man hisself: where he's from, who his people are. And, of course, if I ask anything more, they'll just accuse me of being green with envy. So I just sit and listen till she finally folds up her napkin and flounces off to the parlor, with a calculating grin on her face.

Sometime in the afternoon, her suitor—Mr. Shay Taylor—comes calling, and the two of them run out and buy a cheap diamond ring. Next thing we know, the two run off and get hitched, and the very next day he shows up on the front steps bag and baggage. Sister-woman waits till he arrives before she announces to me that Uncle Fate has given her and her new husband my bedroom. Not so much as a day's notice. Uprooted, and now a strange man in the house to boot! Makes me so mad I'm ready to torch it.

Right off, things started to change. First time Uncle Fate has to wait in line for the bathroom, he accuses me of lounging. I says to him, "I'm waiting for some hot water, Uncle Dear. Clareese and that man have used up every last drop." And then he gets huffy and tells me I'm just as bad—and ain't got the excuse of getting primped for work. Which ain't no reason to go a day without a clean bath. But I just let him go on till he finally frets hisself to sleep in his La-Z-Boy. I know he's gonna need it by the time the Taylors come tromping back through that front door strewing clothes from the hall tree to the dinner table. And sure as I know my name, I know something's wrong with the two of them already. I can read sister-woman like an old shoe.

For the last three days, Clareese had been a nervous mess, kowtowing to that man's every need—like a hospital patient. I just watch and listen, but plain as the nose on your face, they're having problems. And after dinner when the two of them pile up in front of the TV set—leaving me and Uncle Fate with just our tea glasses—I says to him, "I think sister-woman's making a fool of herself, stepping and fetching for that man. It ain't like her. Ain't like her at all." And he looks at me and says I just can't understand the ways of marriage, being an old maid. Which of course, he is wrong. I know what I hear, and I trust my ears. And in the past week, I hadn't heard a squeak out of that bed spring next door. Not that I'm listening, of course, but when you've slept in the same bed for a while, you know its ways. A newly married couple is bound to be heard now and again, and I ain't heard a peep. It ain't the kind of thing I can mention to Uncle Fate, so I just sit on it for now.

So the third week we all spend together, things get a little worse. Miss Clareese has taken to wearing lacy lingerie around the house. Uncle Fate just turns a blind eye to it, except for a sly grin at Mr. Taylor now and then. Of course I know what she's up to, but she could strut through the house butt naked and it ain't gonna get a rise out of that man. I ain't one to spread it, but I knew she was bound to blurt something sooner or later to one of them blabbermouths down at the bank, and just like Henny Penny she'd tell the rest. Not that I gave a damn, mind you, but I have to live in this town too. Sister-woman's finally got herself into something she couldn't assign blame to me for.

And then—well into our third week of strained co-existence— Mr. Taylor suddenly announces that he has to make a trip to Cedarville. Cedarville! The state nuthouse I mentioned earlier. Seems he got a piece of mail demanding he drive down to see about his sister. So I says to Clareese, "Are you going with him? Do you want me to go along?" And she turns to me and says,

"Hell no! They got enough nuts to worry about." Just the kind of nasty remark I might expect, but I wouldn't have gone anyway. Of course she kept it from Uncle Fate the whole time, poor thing. All he seems to do anymore is stare out the window at that damn mimosa tree he named after Clareese. And who the hell ever heard of naming a tree after a person? Seemed *he* ought to be goin' to Cedarville with them.

When they return the next day, to my utter surprise, there in the back seat sits this hollow-eyed, little wisp of a woman all bundled up in a dingy overcoat. A vague, far-away smile slowly cracks across her frail face as she steps from the car and looks up at the house. Like she recognizes it somehow. Someplace familiar. Then out comes a single green suitcase and a canvas tote bag, which Mr. Taylor lugs up the steps and drops on the front porch. Needless to say, I'm shocked by the matter, and sister-woman doesn't bother to explain one word or introduce the poor soul. Only later, when I see her suitcase sprung open in the spare bedroom do I realize we have another boarder. Fresh out of the insane asylum!

Now I ain't one to pass judgment in such matters, but I says to Mr. Taylor, I says, "Do they know that she's gone? I mean, did they release her? She seems mighty distant to me." And he tells me she's cured. Now, cured from what, I don't know—and he ain't telling. So I don't know whether to sleep with my back to the wall or hide all the knives in the house or just what. And Uncle Fate ain't about to say a word to darling Clareese about it. She lets on like it was all decided before they ever made the trip down. And I still ain't heard a squeak out of their marriage bed.

I don't mind saying that this latest development sets me on edge, and I don't know how long I can hold my temper. I can say with conviction that I am not cleaning up behind the three of them anymore, and I tell them so. I says to Clareese, "Missy, if it's your design to drive me out of Uncle Fate's house, you'll need a damn bulldozer because I ain't budging." Then she looks at me and says that Uncle Fate is leaving the house and everything in it to her. Just makes my blood boil! And it would have ended in an all-out cat fight for sure if we hadn't been interrupted by the screaming. Uncle Fate is suddenly running through the house like a madman, yelling at the top of his lungs. We can't get a sensible word out of him. He just keeps repeating over and over, "Lizzie! Lizzie! My darlin' Lizzie!" And pretty soon, down the stairs with a bound comes Mr. Taylor. Uncle Fate bolts from his chair and takes a feeble swing at the man. "My Lizzie! My Lizzie! You took my Lizzie!" he keeps yelling. Mr. Taylor backs way off and stares at us all with quizzical eyes. Then he directs his attention toward the parlor and the picture window, and our eyes follow his. And what we see we cannot believe. There in the distance, Uncle Fate's beloved mimosa tree is bent to nearly breaking point. He accuses Mr. Taylor of the hateful deed because the man once told him that the tree blocks the lovely view of the hills. Of course, Clareese rushes to his defense. She sets about to convince Uncle Fate that I had done it—just to spite him for naming that damn tree after her instead of me. So now he turns on me and tells me to pack my bags. Just like that!

Since I don't have to be told twice, I charge right down to the cellar and haul out Mama's old steamer trunk that Uncle Fate let her store there. I call up my cousin Rita June and say I'm coming for a visit, and she says I'm welcome to stay as long as I want. Very next morning, I've got my old Ford loaded to the hilt—every last rag and stick of furniture I can strap on or force into it. And not a soul there to see me off. Uncle Fate has taken to his room and sister-woman keeps to her filthy, loveless bed. Despite my hate and anger at the bunch of them, however, it must have been a much deeper emotion that caused what followed, for I cannot explain it.

I swear to God I had that car in "Drive" when I put my foot to the pedal. But the next thing I know—BAM, I'm smack up against the trunk of that pitiful mimosa tree, and the impact finishes it off. And there I sit, hiked up on the stump and the whole car entangled in its branches. Needless to say, the crash jars every last soul out of their beds. And when they descend upon me, I don't even try to explain. I just sit there with the radio blaring and wait for the sheriff's department to come and cut me out.

Once loose, I grab my train case out of the back seat and march three blocks down the street, where I catch a bus for Cousin Rita's—leaving the whole damn crazy bunch of them back at the house yelling and screaming and taking my name in vain.

Next thing I hear, Mr. Taylor's other sister, Helen Rose from New Orleans, has piled in on them. Shiftless and crazy as the other one. Sister-woman says she don't care. Why should she? She ain't no better than them. And even though I exact a bittersweet pleasure from the fact that Mama's lavaliere is the only good thing she got out of this marriage, I still say she made her damn bed—cold as it is—let her lie in it! As for me, I wasn't asking Uncle Fate for the time of day. Clareese would have him packed up and living with another relative before the month's out anyway. And when it comes time to cart him off to the old folks home, I ain't doing nothing but call up sister-woman on the phone and tell her to go get him—if she ain't in Cedarville herself. And when she don't show up to take him, *then* he'll see that I was right. Mark my word.

Anyway, she ain't getting a dime from his retirement money neither, because he had asked me to have it fixed where if he had to go into the old folks home, his money would go directly to the home. And I did—the same home as Bert's mama Lulu. His lawyer ain't about to make any changes now that he knows Uncle Fate ain't got good sense anymore. But knowing sister-woman, she'll probably get J.T.'s lawyer to whittle up a case for her. Now them two, they would make a perfect pair—Bonnie and Clyde all over again.

I only mention all this about sister-woman and Uncle Fate because Bert used to be so sweet on Clareese, and Uncle Fate courted mama when they were young. And of course Rita June always reminded me of Mama.

Anyway, it's six solid months till I can find a job and get out on my own. Rita June says I can stay on with her, but to tell you the truth, she's damn near as crazy as sister-woman and her new in-laws. This place may not look like much, but it's all mine. Till next May anyway—but that's another story, and believe me, you

ain't got the time. And I ain't got the best job in the world neither, but they pay me regular. What I do is I answer the phone
over at the Francis Hotel. You see, I have to stay on the line long
enough to be sure they have a good connection and all. And let
me tell you, you wouldn't believe some of the conversations I've
had to listen to. The things I hear—Lord, don't let me get going.

This woman at work keeps asking to rent my other bedroom,
but I tell her I done promised my cousin Rita June—which is
just a small lie, since I did tell Rita I owed her one for taking me
in. To tell the truth, I'm doubling up on my prayers that woman
won't ask no more and stays put, and so far it's working. I ain't
got the stomach for her gibble-gabble. Lord, she never shuts off.
It is a shame there ain't a single soul in this town that's fit for
that bedroom—I could sure use the money. But you probably
know well as I do, they move in on you just nice and tidy as can
be, and next thing you know, the house looks like a storm blew
through it, and they've emptied your cupboards and refrigerator
too. Although, I did try a boarder one time, but she got carted off
in an ambulance one night and I ain't seen her since. Some girl
from out of town, just trying out a new place. That's her rag mess
of clothes over yonder in the corner, still waiting from somebody
to pick them up. I expect I'll end up giving them away to the
second-hand store or maybe the nuns over in Monroe. Oh well,
where were we?

Now this next part, I've got to do some more remembering.
It seems to me that the postmaster has already finished his lunch
at the café when I get there. That part I remember because Tallulah Bunn has him hemmed up on his way out, jacking her jaw
while the man stands there hat-in-hand waiting for her to draw
breath so he can squeeze in a good-bye. And when he sees me
over in the corner, he quick tells her he needs to speak with me
and leaves Miss Tallulah talking to herself on the front steps.
Says he wants to ask me a couple of things, you know. I guess
somebody must've told him I have a good eye and good ear for
the truth, so he plops down across from me in my booth and

introduces hisself some more—all about his kids and the state buildings at the capitol and such. But I know what he's after and I don't flinch from it. I tell him right up front that Bert Dilly ain't got a clear thought yet what he's up against with this post office mess. But I was wrong, at least partly, because what he asks me about first is how come the state or parish hadn't taken over that Pitcher property out there and turned it into an official cemetery. He's very curious about that land. I feel like asking him what the hell business is it of his what happens out there in Pitcherville, but to be honest with you, he seems like a real nice man—just a little nosey. I still don't say a word about it, mostly on account of the hearing going on and all. And *then* he wants to know what is my impression of Bert Dilly's mental state. I just tell him I don't know much about it, but that Bert did come by the crazy part honest. And I may have mentioned something about his mama's high dive into the Gulf of Mexico just to illustrate it—but that's it. I can be mighty tight-lipped.

Anyway, the next thing I know, Mr. Postmaster has invited hisself over to my house for Wednesday supper. All I said was that he ought not take all his meals at Haney's Café—greasiest skillet in three parishes—and he wasn't gonna find a decent mess of fried chicken outside my own kitchen. And sure enough, here he comes knocking at 7:30 sharp, before I can even get my prayer meeting Bible and hat put away. Can you believe it?

I stick him in the parlor with the radio going and have the table set in half an hour—fried chicken, potatoes and gravy, purple hull peas, and hot water bread. And let me tell you, I'm glad I took his word when he said he was hungry. I think this was the first home-cooked meal the man's seen in years. Ate like a field hound. I'm here to tell you, there wasn't nothing left in that plate but tongue tracks. I swear I don't know where he stuck the sweet potato pie and coffee—maybe in his fancy hat.

Then we finally get around to some conversation that ain't already been chewed up—pleasant conversation—and not a word about Bert's sanity hearing. He's ready to move on to other things. Like what I think about that bigmouth Faye Bawcom that squealed on Bert and wrote them nasty letters. And what do I make of all the letter-writing to his office, and did I myself send him any letters—asked real nice and polite, like he is truly interested in what I have to say.

Well hell, that alone should have set me on point. It ain't my habit to discuss my neighbors with just anybody, but I swear that man has such a kind way, I break down and let him in on a little. First I clear the air that I ain't written, called, telegrammed, or so much as hollered in the direction of Baton Rouge—though I did consider it a time or two. I also admit to having heard a bit about it, but I says to him, "I got a full-time job running my own business." Then I look him square in the eye and tell him he's pumping a dry well. Of course, I know the whole story, mind you, but he ain't entitled to it quite yet. He'll have to wait a month or so for that, and even then, only if he drags me in for the federal hearing.

I quick turn the discussion to his family again, not that I'm the least bit interested in him and his wife's marriage problems. It don't last long though, and before I know it, we lapse right back into Stokely and Bert Dilly. The rest of the evening we talk mostly about our little town here: what folks do, how we live our lives; that sort of thing. And we jaw to nearly eleven o'clock. Lord, I thought he was gonna spend the night, and that's where I draw the line. I'm so tired and wore out by the time he leaves, I can't remember a damn thing I said. I do remember piling into bed and saying to myself, "I hope I ain't let any cats out of the bag." I can see now how that man got to the top of the state ladder.

Very next morning I pop out of bed early, scared to death I'll be late and have Judge Fryer string me up in front of everybody. And guess who meets me at the courthouse steps? Mr. Law Man hisself, with a big briar-eating grin he's getting famous for. Has his hair all parted and patted down with enough oil, it throws a glare on my eyes. And he escorts me up the steps and into the building before he tells me he don't like the idea of me entertaining the postmaster.

"Now how's this gonna look if we don't have the present hearing settled before that postmaster starts *his* proceeding?" he says to me. There's a meanness in his voice, so I just flounce off toward the courtroom like I ain't heard a word he just said.

And guess who else shows up in the courtroom—escorted by the bailiff—but the floozy from that old cathouse in Columbia. I guess I forgot to tell you about her. Never met the woman until the night I went to stay with Hannah when she was down sick. Hannah said no, but I said she was deaf. There was something in that house. Something kept making racket in the back.

"Rats, sure as the world," I says to Hannah, and she quick changes the subject. And not five minutes later, there it goes again: *rat-a-tat, rat-a-tat, rattle.* Gave me the willies, if you want to know the truth. And Miss Hannah just sets there with her coffee and teacakes acting like she ain't heard a whisper. So then about ten minutes or so later, here comes Bert sliding in the door, all lit up and just busting a button to tell us about some old cathouse over in Columbia that got raided the night before. Well sir, I cut him off at the pass. I says to him, "Bert, now how did you find that out? Ain't nothing about it in the paper today."

And then he says he got it from the bank. Miss Hannah chimes in wanting to know why he finds it necessary to discuss people we wouldn't think of associating with. Then there it goes again: *rattle, rattle, rat-a-tat* in the back of the house. But Miss Hanna never misses a beat, that one, just keeps right on talking and shaming old Bert for even mentioning such matters in our presence. Like she's royalty or something.

Don't get me wrong, I like Hannah Dilly, but I do think she's being a bit harsh on Bert. And frankly, I'm feeling uncomfortable in the middle of a family squabble. So I says to Hannah, I says, "Dear, you know Bert can't help it. He ain't got a lick of sense." And then I turn to Bert and say, "She can't hold you accountable, can she, Bert?" You know, trying to make light of the matter. But all Miss Hannah does is invite me to button my lip. After that I just tell them both to just have at. And there goes the racket again. Loud enough this time that even Miss Hannah couldn't ignore it. *Rattle, rattle, rat-a-tat.* And when it stops, she lights into Bert again.

At this point, I've just about had it and reach for my purse, when all hell breaks loose in the back of the house. Something hits the floor THUD—and shakes the whole damn house. Bert quick jumps up and starts toward the hallway—me and Hannah in tow. Naturally, I'm keeping one eye on the floor, expecting a rat to pop out and gnaw my leg off. Then, BAM! BAM! And the two of them go flying off in different directions. Hannah knocks me to my knees, clawing her way over me for the front door. Bert flies off into the first bedroom he can find, and they leave me setting cross-legged and panting on the hall floor. And before I can draw myself upright again, a door flies open and here comes Bert and some other creature tearing past me for the front door. Lord, that's the fastest I ever saw that man move in his life.

When I'm finally able to get up again and make my way to the porch, you never saw such a commotion in your life. Hannah is chasing some woman round and round in a circle—with Bert stuck in the middle, like a May Pole. Makes me dizzy just to look. And when the motion finally stops, and I can get a good look at the woman, it is a pitiful sight. I'd never seen so much make-up and false parts on a face in my life. The whole thing just fell out right there in the front yard. Miss Hannah nearly has a stroke.

You see, what happened was, Bert and that sorry K-Billy Bingham had paid a little visit on that old cathouse a few months back—not a *commercial* call, if you know what I mean, but just to satisfy their curiosity. One of them lovely ladies took a shine to Mr. Bert, and being a man—and a fool—he invites her to drop by anytime she's in town. You know, the kind of thing you'd say to a nice stranger on vacation. And when the cops showed up blowing their whistles and rounding all the gals up, she lights out through the woods in nothing but the tacky lingerie she was wearing and thumbs a ride straight to Stokely and her good friend Bert's house.

Come to find out, Hannah knew the whole thing before I ever got there. She'd shut that woman up with a twenty-dollar bill and a promise to kill her if she didn't stay put. And here I'm thinking the whole time she's just ashamed she's got rats. But when we hear the THUD and the BAM BAM, Hannah truly does think someone—or something—else is in the house. What actually happened was, the woman began to get fidgety sitting back there with nothing to do, so she starts trying on some of Hannah's clothes and all. The THUD came when she hit the floor trying to squeeze her big self into a size eight dress. Bruised her up a bit, but not near as bad as what she gets when Miss Hannah sees her wearing one of her Sunday dresses split up the side. Hannah was fit to be tied.

When I left them, they was all still squared off on the front porch. How the woman got back where she belonged, I don't know. But I can tell you for a fact that Bert Dilly told her to drop by again next time she's in town.

That law dog Perry Mason gets wind of Bert and K-Billy's little cathouse escapade and has the floozy dragged all the way back from Dallas, Texas, ready to stick her on the witness stand. But let me tell you, Judge Fryer is not the least bit amused with it. First of all, she shows up in his courtroom late and wearing the most God-awful get-up you ever saw. A bright purple dress cinched up so tight around the bosom, it was a race to see which one popped out first—her bosom or the bailiff's eyeballs. Let me tell you, it tightened the reins on every husband in the courtroom. And naturally she plops herself down right next to me. Can you believe that?

"How do you do, Miss Peep," she says, remembering me from her last little visit to town, like we were old friends or something. And I'm here to tell you, the looks and whispers it draws nearly sends me to the judge's chambers prostrate with humiliation. But I do manage a quiet hello, polite and all. Then I just pretend she ain't really there, which is damn near impossible with the cheap perfume she's putting off. Nearly gags me to tears till they turn on the big ceiling fan and spread the smell for others to enjoy. Whatever it was, I hope to hell she bought the last of it. Damn shame we didn't have some of it to bring Hannah Dilly back to life after she passed out at the first session.

I tell you the stink is so bad it reminds me of the time Clarence Tubb's goats and cows was let loose on the town—tromping down every flowerbed and vegetable patch on their way in. Made their way right into the school houses and churches and stores— you can just imagine the calling cards they left for us to clean up. Nobody could figure out what spooked them and sent them on such a rampage, but there they were, goats eating up every hymn book and spelling lesson in sight—not to mention half the clotheslines in town. And after it was all over and the wild lot of them was herded back home, the courthouse buzzed for months with lawsuits and cuss fights. I myself did not file a suit, but everybody else in town did. Poor old Clarence had to declare bankruptcy and move to Oklahoma. It was a damn shame, too, because he was a real nice man, Clarence.

Well anyway, the judge finally bangs the court to order with his brand new gavel—this one's made out of metal—and everybody slumps back for a long ride. It don't take long to get the first challenge on the floor. Bert stands up and tells the law dog he ain't got a case against him and then invites him over for dinner. Can you believe that? Judge Fryer sits there dumbstruck, not knowing how the hell to respond. And Mr. Law Man—still grinning—says he'd be glad to join old Bert, so long as he clears the house of all the guns and knives. And the judge loses complete control of the courtroom again. Even the Bunn sisters are doubled over with laughter.

It takes five full minutes and a fine apiece for Bert and the law dog before we can proceed again. And when we do, the judge reads off a whole roster of questions that concern him considerably. Things like: What makes a person crazy? Who should decide that? What evidence should be admitted? The kind of things that make it clear that he's in charge and everybody else better have their ducks in a row. I guess this part takes another ten or fifteen minutes with all the theretos and wherefores and thereofs before we can get back down to business. And when we do, sure enough, the judge has decided he wants to hear from every last one of us—why we think we've been called here in the first place.

Let me tell you, I'm surprised to find out half of them still think this hearing is about the post office mess, and the other half say they don't know a thing about Bert's business or that Pitcher land out there. One old soul, Mrs. Hemphill, swears she's never seen the man in her life. Pure fabrication, since she taught him two years in a row when they moved her up to the sixth grade one year. I know it for a fact: I was in his class. So the judge tells her she might want to clear out the cobwebs and get her story straight before he calls her up to the witness stand if it goes to trial. And she tells him not to sass her. "You still ain't too old for me to take my paddle to, Hobart," she says to Judge Fryer.

We all get a laugh out of that. Everybody except Bert, that is. The man is either scared senseless or in a coma. He doesn't twitch a muscle the whole time we're doubled over. When the judge regains control of his court again, he asks Mrs. Hemphill to please forget his comment about getting her facts straight, and there is another round of laughs over that.

Meanwhile, the lawyer man is doing some heavy consulting with J.T., all huddled up like they're plotting a prison break. But Judge Fryer breaks that up pretty quick and asks the man to call anybody he wants to the stand, which is actually a ladder-back chair—something like the one you're sitting in there, only darker. So he calls us all up one by one, firing off questions meant to lead us into some kind of trap. I myself do just fine. I tell him I ain't seen nothing out of the ordinary for Bert. But some of them others—Lordie, what a colorful picture they made of the truth. The Bunn sisters—Miss Tallulah and Opal—launch into a list of grudges they hold against Bert from since their courting days. The elder one, Opal, loses her place in the midst of all her emotions and ends up reciting the Beatitudes. Gets halfway through them practically before Judge Fryer knocks her out of her box with his gavel. And then there's K-Billy Bingham, of course, who does more good for the law dog than he does for old Bert. The law dog asks K-Billy how long he's known Bert Dilly, and K-Billy says: "Fifty years!"

Judge Fryer turns to him and says, "K-Billy Bingham, you ain't but thirty-five years old."

K-Billy scratches his head and says to him: "Then thirty-five years, Your Honor. We was born on the same day right next to each other. His mama, Miss Lulu, and my mama was right there with us." He nods at Bert and then grins real big at the lawyer. The judge throws him off, too, saying he ain't heard so much self-incrimination since the Teapot Dome Scandal. And here they think Bert's the one that ain't got good sense. At least he knows better than to call K-Billy up to the witness stand for his defense.

That hearing goes on for two long days by the time we have to listen to the lawyer man read out loud what he'd been told by the people in this very courtroom—and then listen to him talk about the shame he feels for all of us altering our stories any such way and leaving out important parts. Nearly makes me sick the way he wags his finger at us while he parades around the courtroom with the Bible in his hand. Like Moses when he came down from the mountain to find his people turned heathen.

Next thing we know, him and the judge and Bert and J.T. all step back into the judge's chambers—a little room about 6 x 8 with only one comfortable chair, a cot, and a bookcase—where they converse for half an hour, while the rest of us cross our legs and hope to hold it in. But at least we don't have to watch Miss Hannah being dragged off like roadkill again. Now there's a blessing.

When they finally return, the bailiff calls us all to our feet again and announces his Highness, and we listen to a lot more wherefores and therofs, and finally they call a few more of us up to the stand. And then the judge does something very surprising. He calls up the fat little Catholic postmaster. Nobody can figure that one out, especially since the judge made it damn clear that this hearing has nothing to do with the post office federal hearing coming up. But there he is, big as day.

Miss Darla Birdlace—the crazy one that runs away, you remember—she sticks her hand in the air and leaves it there till Judge Fryer finally calls on her, and he tells her to turn up her hearing aid. She wants to know why he's here at all—"the little satchel-carrying troublemaker." And it damn near lapses into a kangaroo court all over again, till she's told to take her seat, shut up, and don't raise her hand no more today. It takes another half-hour after that to choke testimony out of the little postmaster, mostly having to do with how the books balanced and the record-keeping, and whether or not he's having to clean up a messy trail made by Bert.

But the biggest surprise of all, old man Mojo—who ain't even on the list posted out there on the courthouse door—is called up to the stand. That ain't his real name, Mojo—just a nickname they gave him because he can cast spells, they say, and lives way off in the woods over near the Pitcher place. His real name is Noble Koontz. He only comes into town now and again for tobacco and rum. That's what he drinks on account of he was in the South Pacific Ocean back in WWI. That's where they say he learned to cast spells and cure people. Hell, if he could cure people, he could mop up in this town! But some folks believe it. I myself think he's just another garden variety nut. Says he's seen enough water for a lifetime and can't get far enough onto land and into the woods to suit him.

Mojo was the very first person the district postmaster conversed with that day he came to town. I ought to know. I happened to be right there outside the liquor store when they damn near collided. The man ain't kept company in the past five years. Ain't took a bath in that long neither, if you ask me. And when the postmaster finally moves on down the road, I says to Mr. Mojo, I says, "That's a fine leather jacket you got there, Mr. Mojo. Did you get it mail order?" And he says back to me, "It was my daddy's." And then I says to him, "I guess that postmaster remarked on it as well." He quick says back to me, "Is that what he is? Said he was just visiting here. He a friend of yours?"

Before I can respond, he says to me that the man seemed mighty interested in the folks here in Stokely. Especially Bert Dilly over at the post office. And I ask him polite as can be, "What did you tell him, Mr. Mojo?" He tells me it ain't none of my damn business. "But if you *need* to know," he says, "he asked me how was the mail service here in town."

He said the last part walking away from me and off down the road. I know right then and there Bert Dilly is gonna be hauled into court, because federal folks don't waste their breath for nothing. I also know if the postmaster is pumping for confirmation, he hit a dry well. Mojo don't know one thing about them post office charges or Bert's little mess. At least that was my thought.

But on court day, here he comes, Mr. Mojo, slinking into the courtroom wearing his hunting pants and dirty leather waistcoat. I tell you, you could smell him before you could see him. Didn't even clean hisself up for court. And don't think Judge Fryer don't notice it. He sends Mojo over to the drugstore for either deodorant or some Aqua Velva—his choice. Ten minutes later he comes strolling back in smelling like just another cathouse and up go the windows and hand fans all around.

Judge Fryer puts the lawyer man on hold and calls Mojo up to the stand and explains what's going on to him real slow. The man's travelled around the world on a battleship and ain't never been in court of law in his life. The judge tells him to dress nicer next time and then turns him over to the law dog for questioning.

"Now Mr. Koontz," the lawyer says, but old Mojo stops him right there.

"They call me Mojo," he says gruffly back at the lawyer.

"Okay . . . Mr. Mojo. Have you had any bad experiences here at the Stokely post office?"

Old Mojo just sits there with a smirk on his face and says back to him: "Why? You got somebody you want me to shoot for you?"

Down comes the gavel and Judge Fryer threatens to fine Mojo if he makes one more smart remark. The lawyer man lets him go after that, and Mojo swaggers back over and drops in his seat near the back. A few others are called back up and put through their paces, and then the judge must have hit on something in one of their statements. He calls old Mojo back up to the witness chair and then gets up and walks all the way around to the out-

side and parks hisself right in front of the man. We don't know
if he is gonna bop him on the head with his gavel or just what,
but he stands there awhile, stretching his jaw and scratching his
temple. And then he casts a look over at J.T. and the lawyer man.

"You ever see this man before?" the judge asks Mojo. "The
one sitting right there with J.T. Dilly?"

Mojo eyes the two and takes a long while to answer, and
Judge Fryer starts to ask him again when he blurts out, "Yessir.
Seen them talking together. Twice. Way out there on the Pitcher
place."

The judge raises his brow and proceeds to ask if he was able to
catch anything they said.

"They was talking about clearing that land out there and
sticking houses on it. Right next to the best hunting woods in the
parish! You ain't gonna let them do it, are you, Fryer?"

The judge shoves his eyes back in his head and tells Mojo he
better remember to address him as Judge or Your Honor, and
then tells him to go on.

"They said they couldn't wait to get their hands on that land,
after they get rid of Bert Dilly. Get him declared crazy and
shipped off somewhere or something like that. And Mr. J.T.,
setting over there, says he feels kind of sorry about that part and
couldn't they just settle for taking the family money?" With that,
he shifts to the other hip and asks the judge if he wants to hear
any more, and the judge waves him on. "That one there," he says,
pointing at the lawyer, "he tells Mr. J.T. that some office over in
Monroe is willing to buy that Pitcher land flat out for $5,000.00
quick as they get this hearing closed. And J.T. there nearly busts a
vessel with excitement."

Up jumps the lawyer and J. T. both, objecting to the whole
damn thing, and down comes the gavel again, and the judge gives
them their last warning—they are not to interrupt one more time.
He tells Mojo to continue with his story.

"And then J.T. asks the man there what happened to building
all them houses we been planning together?

"'Oh, that's only if you want to go to all that bother,'" the law man says back to him, 'and have your money tied up so long. I just figured a smart man like you might want your money up front. It could take three or four years to get the building off the ground,' he says. 'Might not even pay off,' he tells J.T."

And then Mojo looks up at the judge, who has returned to his chair, and says to him, "I had my rifle right there in my hands, and let me tell you, at that very moment, I was having a hard time telling a squirrel from a rat. I like to done it for sure—if you know what I mean. Could have shoveled them both into the Pitcher graveyard right there on the spot."

And now it all comes out. When the law dog hears about all them bodies strewn from hell to Hawaii, he's ready to cut and run. What he does—to make it official—is he stands up in front of the judge and declares his intentions of dropping the entire matter. Judge Fryer asks him to explain hisself a bit further before he rides off in a cloud of dust, leaving the good folks here to put things on an even keel again—seeing as how him and J.T. had fanned this matter to a tempest. Naturally, all the two can do is hem and haw some more and point a finger at each other—and I ain't saying which finger.

With that, Judge Fryer asks J.T. if it is his intention to get hisself another lawyer. J.T. is so shocked by this turn of events, he tells the judge he'd just as soon drop the whole damn thing. You should have seen the looks on people's faces—all this buildup and legal falderal, and for what? The judge and every soul in the courtroom is plumb disgusted. Bert pops up out of his chair and tells J.T. he's mean as Cain and got the law devil over that to help him out.

It don't take long for Judge Fryer to finish it up. He tells the law dog he's going to that law office in Monroe next week per-sonally—AND to Hodge—and hand them a copy of the court proceedings. Just so they can see what kind of lawyer they were dealing with. He threatens to hold the both of them for extortion if they say one more word, and I'm here to tell you, J.T. Dilly ain't far behind the law dog getting out of Dodge. Every last person in the courtroom volunteers to help him pack. We don't know if he joined back up with them traveling freaks and misfits or just what. But the funniest thing that come out of all this mess is that the next thing we hear, old Mojo and Aunt Flossie have moved in together out there in the woods next to the Pitcher boneyard.

From what we've heard, the lawyer man has already been run out of three more parishes and moved to Texas, where he probably thinks folks are more ignorant. As for J.T.—hell, he's lucky he ain't stretched out with the rest of them Pitchers out there. It's the only damn way he's ever gonna get a piece of that land.

After it was all said and done, you could tell Bert was sorry for J.T. Poor Bert, sitting there in his blue serge suit every day, fanning his embarrassment. I do believe he would have gave that property to J.T. outright if he'd just gone about it in a decent way. But not Miss Hannah. Whew! She ain't got no more use for J.T. Told me she wouldn't grab a hose if he caught on fire. But none of this seems to linger long—it ain't but a month before Bert has to go to court down in Baton Rouge and deal with the feds.

In the meantime, a lot of things happen. First of all, the letter-writing picks up speed again, and the fat little Catholic is carrying a metal cane. The Bunn sisters make no bones about it— they're ready to lynch the state postmaster. "Him and his laws," they huff. "Hmh!" They ain't the least bit concerned about Bert or what the law says; they just want to know the town gossip without having to ask for it. And the new little postmaster don't give them nothing but their mail. I'll say one thing for that man, he does what he's hired to do. But that don't necessarily make it right in a small town like Stokely—you got to ease up a bit on the letter of the law.

Just like the day I walk into the post office, nice and polite as can be, and ask the man for a pass key to my box, on account of I left mine at home. And he says to me, "Madam, we discussed this the last time you forgot your key. I can't let you in again," he says, smiling at me the whole time. Burnt my butt up! Oh, excuse my language again, but he ain't out one penny opening my box. So I says back to him, I says, "Sir, do you expect folks around here to put up with that attitude? You ain't running Grand Central Station here, you know!" I was fit to be tied. Imagine being kept out of your own mailbox. Don't sound legal to me. He just shrugs his round little shoulders.

Well, after I huff out and finally catch my breath, I hightail it home and fire off a three-page letter to the state postmaster's office myself—not about Bert Dilly—about the fat little Catholic too big for his tight little britches. And I don't crowd it up with a bunch of lies neither. I tell him how ruffled up the man's got everybody here in Stokely, and then I tell him I hope he's planning on coming to Bert's hearing in Baton Rouge.

Bert has no idea the lengths folks are going to to get him back into the post office. Even the mayor buckles under the pressure and sends off a high-toned appeal to the state postmaster. Everybody and their grandma has the phone lines popping and snapping with huffy calls to anybody they think might get old Bert off—everybody except the town clergy. This is where they draw the line. It's one thing to forgive, they say, but they are not about to compromise their morals by making excuses or misuse their holy positions in such a way. All except for Reverend Dinker, of course. That man had never been behind a popular cause in his whole life, and this is a golden opportunity to get a little glory. The most he'd ever been able to influence public opinion was the time he fasted for a week to get former Mayor Belvin's picture off the "Welcome to Stokely" sign, which depicted the mayor posing on top of a cloud above St. Paul's Church—as if God could give a damn about politics in Stokely. Any ambitions the reverend had for prominence flew south when he pulled that little stunt. Barely makes a living in the pulpit these days—damn near starves from Easter to Christmas season. Good thing his wife's got that teaching job over in Hodge.

As it turns out though, we think Reverend Dinker might be a good person to have on the team. It seems that before he moved to Stokely, his wife, Selma, went to school with the wife of the state postmaster. And Miss Selma is certainly not above the daily hear-tell herself. It irks her to no end the way the preacher-men turn their backs on poor Bert, knowing good and well they listen to every piece of juicy gossip their saintly wives drag in.

One morning, off she traipses to Baton Rouge to see her dear friend Caprice Upshaw—the state postmaster's wife. All by herself! And two days later, here she comes tearing back into town with a pouty smirk on her face and not a kind word for anybody. She later tells Shirley Bailey at the Beauty Barn that *Miss Caprice* has become so high and mighty with her husband's state job that the whole visit she just strutted around like a peahen, putting on airs. Told Selma, "I'll have to think it over." And then just before she left—when Miss Caprice hadn't pledged her support—Selma got mad and told her where she could get off.

Well, when the state postmaster gets wind of his wife's meeting with Selma, he tells Miss Caprice she's as good as tampered with evidence and now he can't even testify to what he had heard hisself from me or anybody else in Stokely. How we find out about the postmaster's dilemma is nothing short of providence. It seems Miss Caprice, in anger at her husband, dashed off a letter to Alene Belcher over in Jonesboro, a letter telling her the whole thing—in confidence, of course—Alene being her closest, dearest friend. But Miss Alene don't let her coattail touch her butt till she calls up Selma Dinker on the phone and reads the whole letter to her word-for-word. Of course, she knew she could trust Selma to never let a word slip. After all, Selma's a good Christian and the wife of an Episcopal priest. The whole town could recite you that letter by heart before the sun set.

The days drag on and poor Bert don't sleep a wink between the two hearings. And Miss Hannah just struts around town pretending ain't none of it happening. She drops all her church duties at Christ Methodist and joins up over at Reverend Dinker's Episcopal church. Says to me, "He's the only sane man left in this town." And that was mighty damn funny coming from her. Just two weeks earlier he was an "idol worshiper—like them Catholics." To tell you the truth, I myself don't trust any church that ain't got at least a few crosses and pictures of Jesus on the walls, amen. But I don't give a damn if people wear Jesus on the cross in a loincloth or a plain cross polished to a glare. I ain't noticed any one of them sprouting wings—congregations that is. Like as if God set us all up like toy soldiers and said have at it.

I've failed to mention one person who probably knows Bert well as anybody, but I knew they'd never get her to Baton Rouge. She was always sweet on Bert, but he never did a thing to encourage it. Neither did Miss Hannah. She always said Ivy Webb was plumb *curious*—which probably sounds funny to you now that you know a bit about the Dillys themselves. "She's spiteful," Hannah would tell everybody. One day when we was kids, Clay Birdwell decided to shave off Ivy's cat's tail, and the very next day Clay's dog Buster went missing—ain't nobody seen that dog since.

Miss Ivy turned inward after her mama and daddy died and left her alone in the world. Just took it into her head one day to do some traveling, and the next thing we know, she's trotted off to Paris, France, all by herself. A month later she returns with a small painting of her and some man on that river that runs through it—the Seine. And of course, the ring she kept shoving in everyone's face. "Not an engagement ring," she says to us, but you could tell by the way she batted her eyes and tossed her hair she wanted everybody to think it was—especially Bert. Something to keep folks guessing, I suppose, like we had nothing better to do than sit around speculating on her pitiful life. She used up a lot of her savings on that one wild hair and didn't have nothing to show for it except a painting you could barely make out. But I knew there'd be a story somewhere behind that picture.

She kept saying that the man in the painting—the one that gave her the ring—was coming to see her. "A world traveler," she said to us, "a rich widower from Chicago." Bank president or something—she was a little vague on that part. Of course, we didn't pry. Bad enough we thought she was lying, but to trap her in it wouldn't be Christian. We'd have all been glad to just forget the whole damn thing, except she kept telling everybody the man was coming in on an afternoon plane to Monroe. Of course, it left us all wondering what kind of made-up mishap would keep him from getting here. "If she's half smart" somebody said, "she'll say the man broke his leg back in Chicago. Or have him run over by a bus. Anything less and somebody would catch her in a lie." Folks talk, as you well know.

Sure enough, five o'clock comes and goes with no sign of the man. A cool breeze moves in bringing neighbors to their front porches, and just before the edge of night, a big yellow Chrysler comes cruising up the lane. Sure enough, it circles and lights right in front of Miss Ivy's house. A tall man crawls from the driver's seat and straightens the cap on his head—the kind of cap they wear to play golf, a bright plaid.

It was a long walk up to the door, and he seemed to stretch it out—stopping now and again to tip his hat at the neighbor ladies on their porch swings. Naturally, Miss Ivy is shut up inside, not about to give the least impression she's sitting on the doorbell. Just coy as you can imagine, she lets that man ring the bell ten times before she decides to answer it. And then one hour later, here comes her suitor out the front door again, tipping his hat to the same nosey neighbors who'd sat right there waiting on him. J.T. used to call on the poor thing, too—before he ran off with that freak show. Even K-Billy Bingham took her to a picture show one time, only she got sick half way through it and gave K-Billy the heave-ho. Like I said, she was only interested in Bert.

Next morning, the man drives up in the fancy yellow car again. He struts up the walkway with a big grin on his face, and old lady Gaines is quite smitten when he compliments her daylilies. She'd have had that man in—mark my word—if *Mr.* Gaines hadn't been around. And not five minutes later, here they come—him and Ivy—swinging a picnic basket. He let the top down on the car, and they roar off down the road like a couple of teenagers.

In the meantime, Kettie Lee, the second nosiest old biddy in town, gets on the phone with her cousin in Chicago, who looks up the man in the phone directory. "There ain't a T. Dodd Sellers in the whole book—white pages or yellow!" her cousin says. So naturally, Kettie feels it's her Christian duty to tell all the neighbors, and by the time Miss Ivy returns in the evening, everybody on the street is posted at their front stoop. Of course, the man has no idea what the nosey bunch is whispering about—*chattering* more like. Miss Ivy wouldn't invite him in so late, though they do linger on the porch awhile.

Next morning, they're off again, this time swinging a suitcase and hatbox. Miss Ivy's dressed fit to kill and smiling like a mule eating briars. No doubt about it—the man is taking the poor thing for a ride. Deena Tucker tails them far as the parish line, where she's cut off by a train, and next thing we hear, they've hopped a plane out of Monroe to who knows where. Some say Hollywood. Others say Chicago.

Three months goes by, and old lady Steeple gets a picture postcard from Paris, France. Actually, Bert gets it first, like always, and every soul in town knows what it says word-for-word. Not much to look at, just a bunch of tiny scenes and some French writing. And then last Christmas, she gets another card, with the following words: "Magnifique! Just grand. Think I was made for here!" And that's the last we hear from the woman for a long while. "Just grand, my fanny," Hannah Dilly says to me. "She's been hoodwinked if you ask me, the clabber-headed fool."

Meanwhile, her house sets empty and the grass grows high, but everybody keeps a close eye on it. Come July, her Mr. Sellers rolls into town all by hisself one hot afternoon in another fancy rented car—all hush-hush—then disappears quick as he came. "Miss Ivy's husband," the banker tells us, "came to transfer the rest of her savings." Every last dime her daddy left her when he died.

Folks pawed at the courthouse door—like they always do—trying to find out about this so-called husband and Miss Ivy's whereabouts. They were told sternly that they had no right to her personal business—even if she had no family. But Sybil Leach, one of the tellers, let it slip that her daddy had held on to a bunch of stock shares since before the Depression, and this just fueled more suspicion.

Before we know it, Miss Ivy's house and all its contents—
except for the appliances and a few personal things—go on the
sale block. Folks snatch up everything they can get their hands
on for pennies on the dollar, and two weeks later, a woman with
the eight meanest kids you ever saw moves in and proceeds to
take the damn place apart. It seems Mr. Sellers had changed
his mind about selling Miss Ivy's house after all. Thought he'd
hold onto it for an investment—keep it rented out. It makes the
neighbors so suspicious, they get a lawyer over in Monroe to track
down Ivy Webb and let her know personally what's happening
here. And, sure enough, the lawyer posts a letter to somewhere in
Chicago, which is forwarded from there. But it doesn't reach Ivy
for a month, and by that time, the bandits have fled in the night,
taking all her appliances with them. She wouldn't have one thing
left to set up housekeeping if she finds herself dumped and crawl-
ing back home. Just like when Uncle Fate turned me out—you
remember that.

Well, the days tick by and of course all her neighbors shake
Bert down for information every time they're at the post office.
Then one day the lawyers get in touch to let us know Miss Ivy
was not aware of the situation back here, just that her husband
told her not to worry her pretty head about business things. But
this was hardly the biggest news. We're shocked to a fare-thee-
well to learn that Miss Ivy herself had to respond to the letter
because it seems her husband, Mr. Sellers, had just died unex-
pectedly—a tragic fall from a Paris balcony. Bert Dilly offers to
pay her way back to Stokely hisself, but the lawyers assure us that
Miss Ivy had taken out life insurance on him and her both.

Well, this certainly is enough shock to go around and
keep tongues wagging for a while. Miss Ivy does all her griev-
ing privately, right there in Paris, France, too ashamed to face
us—we assume. And there she stays another long year. It must
have been comforting, some thought, to plan her first visit back
home. Everybody agrees not to say one word about that suspicious husband of hers while she's here. Ain't no use in getting
her all upset again.

And I mean to tell you, we're all popeyed when she shows up with another one of them Paris paintings—her and some *other* man posing next to the Eiffel Tower. I guess joy had finally returned to her life. "A world traveler," she says to us again. "A rich widower from New Orleans." Everybody just smiles and carries on about her fine new clothes and jewelry and her Paris hairdo—*and* her new suitor beside her in the painting. Somehow, I feel myself strangely drawn into that silly picture, lost to it. I just keep staring at it, studying the two of them posing and smiling back at me—just like the one with her first husband—till my mind hears a faint voice somewhere and far off whispering: *That poor old fool.* And the last we heard she'd done widowed again.

Yessir, Ivy Webb could sure tell you anything you want to know about Bert Dilly, being sweet on him since they was kids. Always said if she can't have him nobody can, and given her marriage history, I'd say old Bert dodged a bullet. But you might could write her a letter if you want more information.

How's your tea? I got some more of them fresh teacakes I made yesterday. You might need some refreshments before I tell you about the trip to Baton Rouge. Trip to Hell, more like. It wasn't really a trial, you know. Just another hearing, they said. But none of us really knew the difference—they all look alike. Lordie, you should have been there at 2:00 a.m. when the caravan leaves town for Baton Rouge. Crooks could have robbed us all blind with everybody out of town. I don't think half the houses in Stokely have locks on the doors. You can't get away with nothing in this town. Somebody's always watching.

I swear, every nut in the parish met up at the schoolyard and boarded trucks, cars, station wagons, even two old school buses— must've been fifty vehicles in that caravan. Them buses don't take distance travel well, and one of them has a flat ten miles out of town, and that puts us behind—that and trucks stopping every time somebody bounces off the back-end. And of course there's the car-sickness and bathroom stops. Once, when the bus got up to sixty-five, Noleen Shaker pops her window open to throw up, and the suction snatches her wig right off her head and leaves her looking like a peeled onion. To tell you the truth, I was ready to hitchhike the last fifty miles to get away from the racket and the smell. I would've drove my old Ford, but it's all it can do lately to make it to the church house and back.

When we finally come spitting and sputtering into town, I mean to tell you, they are not ready for us. For one thing, there ain't no parking in front of the courthouse like in Stokely. So we circle around and around and around the block till the rest of us all get car sick, and can't find a single place to pull over. I suspect we'd be circling for a landing to this very day if somebody hadn't bailed out and asked some people where the hell folks park their cars for court. And it don't please one soul when they point us toward a big two-story parking garage three blocks away. They charge you two dollars a day to park and hike in. Thought I was gonna have to puke in my new green organza hat before it's all over. I guess they never saw anything like us before, the way some of them gawk and point. Before we can ever roll to a complete stop, though, here comes Noleen Shaker stomping up the aisle of the bus, demanding the driver turn right around and take her back to find her cheap wig. Poor pitiful thing, she pitches the biggest fit you ever saw. But the driver just keeps right on driving till he finally gets tired of her racket and turns around and says to her: "Hell no! I can't make all these people be late for court just because you didn't tighten down your helmet before you boarded my bus!" So she stomps back to her seat and sets there the rest of the day. Frankly, we're all glad; she threw up on several of us. I tell you, I shudder to even think about the ride back home. No sir, this place is not ready for us.

When we finally make it to the courthouse without getting clipped by traffic, every last soul makes a beeline for the bath-rooms. You should have seen the line out and around the corner, all of us standing there smelling like puke in our cheap jewelry and gaudy get-ups—looks like we just blew in from the Mardi Gras. The courthouse clock strikes nine o'clock and we're still lined up. Pretty soon, here comes a bailiff—a *real* bailiff, starched uniform and everything—and he starts asking us what time our court date is. So we tell him 9:30, and he asks us which case. I guess there must have been a dozen scheduled for the day, and he offers to escort us all to the right room. When he gets a good whiff of the crowd, he don't say one more word about us being late—just moves off upwind of us.

The first impression I get from the courtroom, once we get in and get seated, is that it don't look a thing like the ones I've seen in the movies. Bigger flags and pictures of famous men on the walls, and the room is divided into sections by short fences with swinging doors—that part I did see in a movie once.

The judge, a Mr. Roger Huff, tells us all to be seated, and the fancy bailiff stands off to the side with his arms crossed. The first thing the judge tells us is that this is an *open hearing* and then explains what that means to us. Since it involves the whole town of Stokely, they have to make room so everybody that wants can be heard. And they sure got a turnout! Looking around the room, I wouldn't blame the judge if he sent the whole lot of us back home to wash up and change clothes and try again. All I keep seeing in my mind is Noleen sitting out there pouting and smelling up the whole bus. Somebody offered her a kerchief to tie up her head—ugliest rag you ever saw, not much better than nothing—and she just takes it and chucks it out the window.

While I'm sitting there, I suddenly think to myself: *Lord, ain't nobody even mentioned the little episode about Bert renting out that postal box to the out-of-towner.* You need to hear about this one. I guess it was about a year or so ago when this man drove up to the post office one day to see about getting a mailbox. Said he lived over in Chatham and their post office was slap out of boxes, and he was in a rush to get an address where he could receive his mail and all. So Bert—after a fair amount of questioning—gives him the key to a box, and he sets sail.

A solid week goes by, according to Bert, and not a slip of mail comes for the man. And then another week passes and still no mail, and then a month is up and ain't a thing arrived. So Bert gets on the phone and calls up the number the man wrote on the box rental card and some woman answers and says she don't know any Joe Barker and please don't bother her no more. So naturally Bert calls the number again, thinking he must've dialed it wrong, and the same woman picks up and tells him to take a hike. And then the very next day, a green envelope arrives at the post office from Shreveport, smelling like perfume—certainly not a regular envelope, but not like a birthday card neither. Bert first sticks it in the man's box and then he suddenly remembers—after all this time—that he ain't supposed to issue them boxes to nobody but citizens of Stokely. You see what I mean about Bert?

So there he is, stuck with a piece of mail for somebody that ain't even supposed to be there. What he does then is get on the phone with the postmaster over in Chatham to see if he knows the man—the town being so small and all—and the postmaster says he never heard of him and Bert should just hold on to it till the man comes in for it.

And if this ain't strange enough, two days later, here comes a pretty young thing dressed up fit to kill and sticks a key in that box. The office is especially crowded just then, and by the time Bert can get over to where she was, she's out the door and bar-reling toward West Monroe. But the suspicion don't stop there. Very next day, a big package arrives for Mr. Joe Barker, a big heavy box—and guess who comes sashaying into the office to get it but that same young floozy. Only this time she's got a man with her—youngish like her and handsome as a movie star. They march right over and get in line to see the postmaster, and let me tell you, Bert drops everything else right there on the spot. Turns old lady Beene over to Nita Rae and nearly hops the coun-ter—Nita Rae told me that part herself. And the next thing she knows, he's escorting the two into his office in the back. Bert can be very accommodating, as you already know, but he ain't nearly 'bout prepared to deal with a city woman like her. She not only gets away with the key and the big box—but a big bucktooth grin from yours truly as well.

To make a long story short, this goes on for four months—her coming in and snatching up boxes and disappearing—and no sight of Mr. Barker at all. Until one Friday morning—I remember that day—the man shows up asking about getting a bigger box. Says he's started a business and needs to keep his personal affairs separate, so he really needs *two* boxes. Well, Bert tells him he ain't got no more boxes, and he needs to get his name on a list over at the Chatham station and wait for somebody to move or die. And that's the wrong thing to say—because the fit hit the shan! The man yells and cusses and swears he'll be back with his lawyer. You've never seen such ranting and raving. I was right there when it happened. Of course, I'd already taken cover over in the corner with old lady Beene and her parasol when he finally storms out the door again. Here he is using Bert to bend regulations and then threatens to sue him.

After that little episode, I'm getting a little suspicious myself, so I don't do nothing but go home and call up the operator over in Shreveport and ask for the number of a Joe Barker, and she says, "Home or business?" I ask for both—not really thinking about calling either one, mind you. But I suspected something ever since the first time that young floozy flounced into the post office—something unnatural and fast about her and that young man with the flashy eyes. I just knew them two was up to no good, and sure enough, a few days later, here comes a state patrol car with a couple of well-heeled gentlemen in dark suits and sunshades. They march into the post office and pull Bert outside to talk. Quiet and efficient as you please. And the next thing we know, they clean out Mr. Joe Barker's box and grab his parcels from Bert's office and blow out of town fast as they came in.

It seems our Mr. Barker had been using his Stokely mailbox to run a business alright, but certainly not one you could discuss in decent company. Let's just say him and the young floozy and her boyfriend with the Hollywood teeth were distributing dirty magazines all over five parishes—and making a damn tidy living at it, too. They figured they didn't need to worry about a small town postmaster like Bert figuring it out—and they was right! But I have to tell you, it does make me wonder why Bert hadn't peeked inside some of that mail. Hannah says he probably did and liked what he saw. I can't believe it because him or that blabber-mouth K-Billy Bingham would've had it all over town.

Anyway, that's what preoccupies me when I first get seated in the Baton Rouge courtroom. Lord, Bert don't need any more to answer for than what he's got now. Pretty soon, I spot Reverend Dinker and Selma coming in the double doors, cool and fresh as you please from their drive down in her pink Buick. I keep craning my neck to see if I can spot her dear friend Caprice Upshaw, the state postmaster's wife, in the crowd. Not that I would know her on the street—just that she might stick out in a room full of people I do know. I picture her all gussied up like a movie star and wearing a fur jacket and lots of jewelry. Funny the things you think of while you're killing time.

Next thing we know, in marches Bert in his blue serge suit again—all by hisself, except for the bailiff that shows him to his seat. We still can't believe he refuses to get hisself a lawyer. Stubborn as a cowlick, that one. And not even Miss Hannah here to give him a little moral support. I don't think that woman will ever darken a courtroom again after fainting and falling out with her dress hiked up back in Stokely. It's a good thing Bert's mama is laid up in the old folks home, I say to myself. But everybody else is there, even the mayor and his wife, setting way in back off to the side.

All the while, Bert's panning the room, squinting and bug-eyeing, trying to see who all showed up. He ain't talked to nobody in a week, and that ain't like him at all. Broke his heart every time he passed his post office, till he finally just avoided Main Street altogether. And here he is, setting up there by hisself now. I must say, his blue serge looks as good as the one the lawyer they assigned him is wearing.

The judge is about to say something finally when he's interrupted by a loud THUD from the back of the room. We all turn around with him just in time to watch K-Billy Bingham pulling hisself up off the carpet floor. The clumsy fool tripped over his own feet lumbering down the aisle and went sliding. We ain't never seen him in that zoot suit before, and frankly, I don't know what the hell got into that man. You can tell he'd bought it some time ago, on account of the way the stripes all curve going up his legs and arms from being stretched out by all the weight he's put on—like trying to force ten pounds of crap into a five-pound bag. Wouldn't surprise me to see he ripped the rear-end right out of them pants when he did the splits. And I got to tell you, the judge is not happy with the commotion. No sir, but folks ain't about to double over with fun in *his* courtroom. We ain't in Stokely anymore.

After a fair amount of chit-chat with the lawyer and the state postmaster and the little Catholic postmaster from Stokely and a few other people we ain't ever laid eyes on, Judge Huff turns his attention back to the rest of us. I turn to Charlene Little and says to her, "I think we're riding a spooked horse here. Just look at Bert over yonder twitching and nodding and scratching. They may not let him go this time." She just shakes her head and whispers back, "Amen!" Of course she ain't got no room to talk, with them damn young'uns of hers ripping up and down the streets at all hours on their stolen bikes. Only reason she's here is that the Bunn sisters—who parked themselves right behind me, by the way—put her up to complaining to anybody that would listen. Then Tallulah Bunn leans forward and tells us to shush. I ain't been shushed since I was sixteen, and let me tell you, it's all I can do to keep from turning around and painting her face with a palm print. They might be high and mighty back in Stokely, but we're in Baton Rouge now.

Anyway, I keep my mouth shut once the proceedings get started in earnest. The first order of business is to listen to the alleged charges, and this takes about an hour—with even more wheretos and therefores and some new ones we ain't ever heard of. Somewhere about in the middle, Judge Huff calls a fifteen-minute recess and everybody stampedes out like a herd of mad cows—back to the bathrooms, most of them—leaving Bert almost by hisself in the courtroom. I make my way down close as I can and tell him he looks real nice in his blue serge, and he smiles back at me. I bet every time he looks over at all the loose cannons in this courtroom, he wishes some of us had stayed home.

It reminds me of the time back before the Depression when Mama took me to the parish fair one day, and she made me wear Clareese's red dress. She had to stay home on account of sneaking out at night and lying to Mama. If Daddy had been home, she'd have gotten to go anyway. I was just a couple of years older than her, but my body had begun to sprout out in new directions, and her red dress cut me tight at every curve. Mama said it looked fine, but then she didn't have to wear it. So there I am walking down the midway, gasping for air in precious Clareese's tight red dress, when guess who should come charging toward us but a gang of girls from my class, arm-in-arm, biting at cotton candy and sniggering. You know, I should've expected it. I found out later that sister-woman told them to look me up at the fair if they wanted a good laugh. I must have ran into every kid in my school that day.

Mama just ambles along humming to herself, taking in all the sights and sounds and daydreaming about other times and other fairs. But let me tell you, I could have died that day. That's how come I know what's going on in Bert's head—wishing some of us had stayed home. I could almost feel that way about K-Billy in his zoot suit, too, but to tell you the truth, I don't think he even notices people staring at him. So I ask you, what's the pity?

When we all get back in the courtroom, the judge enters and we all stand up again and sit down again. I tell you, if my mind wandered off even for a minute, I'd swear I was back at St Barnaby's, with all the popping up and down in our chairs. I keep waiting for the judge to order us to kneel.

This time we start by listening to some more gibble-gabble from the postmaster's lawyer, a squeaky little man with a pointy nose and cheesy little moustache and these off-set, beady eyes the color of mud. His name is Mr. Smelt, and he's wearing a white pinstripe with a kerchief in the pocket like that man on my new Sylvania television set, the one in all them car commercials. You can tell he ain't from around here by his accent, and he looks more like he belongs in that car lot than this courtroom. And he has this annoying habit of rubbing his hands together, like the back legs of cricket—like he's itching for your attention. Hell, anybody can tell when he's in the courtroom by the smell of his aftershave lotion. Reminds me of the perfume Bert's lady friend from that cathouse was wearing the day I met her. But to tell you the truth, it don't smell no worse than the creams and lotions and cheap perfumes folks around me are using to disguise the vomity stench we wore in from the trip down here.

He's a tricky little devil, this lawyer—having Bert stand up every time he asks him a question. Bert ain't the standing up type in these kinds of situations. He's fine in Stokely gatherings, but you can't stick him out there center stage in a strange place. No sir! He ain't got the gumption to deal with it. Hell, we can barely hear his answers till Judge Huff tells him to speak up so the court reporter can get it all down on his machine.

The next round of business, Judge Huff explains he's gonna let the lawyer start calling us up one at a time. He says the lawyer and Bert both can ask us questions, since Bert is representing hisself. And pretty soon we're in full swing, and the federal lawyer proceeds to march up and down the room in front of us talking to the floor. And every once in a while, he turns and flashes us a big yellow smile.

First person he plucks from the audience is Reverend Dinker—which shocks our drawers off, since Faye Bawcom is the main cause of all this. And he plows right into Bert's church attendance and the reverend's opinion on Bert's character. Every question he starts out with, "What can you tell the court about such and such." The reverend holds tight and picks his words careful-like. His wife sits back there either nodding or screwing up her face each time he answers. "What can you tell the court about Mr. Dilly's relationship with the folks of Stokely? What can you tell us about the order of business at the post office when he was there?" This last part brings a strained look over everyone's face. And Miss Faye sets there with her head under her arm.

But this is nothing compared to the questions he fires off at Tallulah Bunn when she flounces up to the stand. But before she gets there, the judge motions over to Bert that it is his turn to ask any questions. The old fool just waves back to him, no idea what the hell to do at this point. The judge explains to him again. "Mr. Dilly," he says in a deep, sober voice, "Mr. Dilly, you filed papers to represent yourself in this court. Now, represent!"

So Bert wobbles to his feet and yells across the room, "Reverend Dinker, have I ever been late getting your mail in your box?" Then when the reverend answers no, Bert sits back down and tells the judge he ain't got no more questions.

Dumb as a stump, like I said before. I can't for the life of me figure out why that judge don't just call another recess and order Bert to quick find hisself a real lawyer. With that, the reverend is let go and the lawyer calls up Miss Tallulah again. She ain't happy because she's already made one trip up there, only to be sent back to her chair. And let me tell you, that one set the store on fire.

"What can you tell us about the way Mr. Dilly ran the post office in Stokely, Miss Bunn?" You'd think the jaws of Hell opened. She spends ten full minutes griping about the way Nita Rae sometimes makes folks wait in line while Bert is in the back shaking and jarring and feeling everybody's mail before he sticks it in their box or hands it to them. And then she lights into some gossip put about town that he's read her postcards and held her letters up to the window light to try to read them. And after ten more minutes—when we think she's finally through—we realize she's just clearing her throat. You can look up "hypocrite" in the dictionary and there's Miss Tallulah. She knows damn well she and her lard-butted sister, Opal, go to that post office every day at two o'clock sharp for their daily doses of hear-tell from Bert. If there is any gossip put about, them two are prime suspects. But when the law devil turns her over to Bert, he just stands up and smiles real big at Tallulah and tells her she picked out a lovely dress to wear down here to his hearing, and he ain't got no questions for her.

The squeaky little lawyer looks like he's about to pee his pants when he sees how Bert plans to handle hisself. It looks like it almost puts him a little off his guard. I know he ain't never encountered anything this strange before, and he ain't quite sure what to make of it. But he don't let that stop him calling up the next person, and Nita Rae Potter tiptoes her way up to the hot seat. She and Bert exchange smiles and gestures and gawk at each other like two people in love. Meanwhile, the little lawyer is rifling through his files for something or other. When he finally finds it, he steps around right in front of Nita Rae, blocking her from rest of us. We don't hear the first question he asks her and up goes Darla Birdlace's hand. The judge sees her and motions for her to lower it, but she don't pay him any mind. She goes right on flapping and waving till Judge Huff interrupts the lawyer and asks her with a scowl what she wants. She says to him, "I can't hear that little lawyer man. Can you turn up his volume for me?"

I don't have to tell you how the judge feels about that. She is escorted out of the courtroom by the bailiff and hurried off to another room by a woman bailiff, who is told to knock some sense into her before she brings her back into his courtroom. And after that little episode, it's clear to us all that this judge don't suffer fools lightly. Miss Darla don't interrupt the judge anymore that day.

Like I told you before, Nita Rae Potter is the salt of the earth. Good as gold. But for all the fine work she's done over at the post office, she ain't got all the dots on her dice neither—which probably explains why she and Bert have got on so well.

"So, Miss Potter, what can you tell the court about Mr. Dilly's habits at the post office?" the lawyer asks her. It takes that woman five full minutes to work up a thought to share, and then all she does is talk about the way folks always insist on conversing with Bert directly instead of her. It goes on from there about, like her first hearing testimony back in Stokely—what she knows about record-keeping matters and such—and she manages to dodge his bullets pretty good. But I can tell you for a fact: that woman ain't never had so much color in her face as when the law devil has her on the hot seat that day.

And after he cuts her loose, he calls up Miss Trixie Devine—
Bert's little friend from the cathouse over in Columbia. And she
faints dead away. No surprise to me, the way she's been white-
knuckling the wood railing in front of us. Her suitcase purse hits
the floor with a loud THUD and everybody looks around to see
where K-Billy hit the floor again. I know these people think we
ain't never seen a courthouse in our lives, the way we gape and
stare and fall out on the floor when we hear our names called out.
Miss Trixie has a lot more in that purse than just a compact and
cheap perfume. I like to never got it off the floor when the bailiff
pulls her over the rail. And we all know this ain't the first time
the woman's been called before a judge. Hell, you'd think she'd
be used to it in her line of work.

And when they finally bring her around and stick her up on
the witness stand, the lawyer wants her to tell the court what her
connection is to Bert Dilly, and does she ever do business out of
the Stokely post office. To be honest, she looks pretty weak and
harmless, even setting up there in that overflowing dress—like
a little girl dressed up all floozy-like. But the federal lawyer,
he takes no pity on her at all. He reads off a list of her former
court appearances—in several parishes—and tries to corner her
into telling him she's been running something illegal out of the
Stokely post office with Bert Dilly's knowledge. I don't know
where in the world he got such an idea. And I don't think he's
allowed to dredge up past history like that, but the judge gives
him a free rein.

Well, that does it. Up pops Bert like a jack-in-the-box and
walks right up to the lawyer man and tells him real loud he ought
to be ashamed of airing that woman's wash in front of us all. And
then he turns to the judge and proceeds to tell him all about how
him and K-Billy Bingham came to know Miss Trixie and all—
until the gavel comes down, leaving Bert and the lawyer and Miss
Trixie all three hanging off his bench. After that, Judge Huff
orders the lawyer to either change the direction of this questioning or move on to the next person. I guess the law devil must've
believed Trixie and Bert, because he kicks her out of the hot seat

and the judge sends her out of the courtroom again to pull herself together. She never really does. And I have to tell you, she whimpers and whines her way through the whole rest of that hearing, setting right next to me.

Next, the lawyer man calls up K-Billy Bingham—and this is another jolt to us all, since we been holding our breath waiting for him to get Faye Bawcom on the hot seat. Somebody has to nudge K-Billy awake when they call his name, and he tromps all over everybody's feet with his number 19s, making his way to the aisle. If there is anybody who can throw that beady-eyed little lawyer for a loop, it's K-Billy Bingham. First of all, the lawyer probably thinks the man's wearing that zoot suit get-up to poke fun at the court. The way the judge fixes his eye on him as he approaches, I know he's plumb disgusted. After all the swearing in and introductions, the lawyer tells K-Billy to look straight over at Bert and hold it while he asks him a question or two.

"What can you tell the court, Mr. Bingham, about the time you and Mr. Dilly here were fired from the meat plant over in Stokely?"

Bingo! Everybody thinks this is the end for Bert Dilly as a free man. K-Billy stutters and stammers around, trying to loosen up a sensible response, but all he comes out with is: "Boy. That's been so long, I forgot we worked there. Now, what was the question?"

Judge Huff's gavel hand gives way and plops down on the bench top. He looks over at K-Billy and lets out his frustration with one stern warning: "One more time, and you're in contempt of court. Thirty days and a fine."

After that, K-Billy's memory improves considerably, and he tells the court every last detail about them going through people's files at the plant. Before the judge can stop him, he spits out a fair amount of personal information on folks setting right there in the courtroom. Things like Toby Finn's little drinking problem and Carl Martin's piles and Brock Nilson's hernia operation over in Shreveport. Granted this all happened twenty years ago, but two of them men are still alive and setting right here listening to it broadcast to the whole courtroom.

BANG goes the gavel again, and Judge Huff asks the squeaky little lawyer if he has anymore questions. To tell the truth, if he does, he's plumb forgot them when the bang of the gavel nearly knocks him off his feet. The judge orders K-Billy back to his seat and stares at him the whole time it takes him to resettle. I know that judge is thinking to hisself that he ain't gonna get no useful information out of that simple-minded fool. Besides, it ain't K-Billy's hearing.

Well, we sit through three more testimonies that day—Earl Rice, Joe Moon, and Crete Waller. Earl does pretty good. He says he can't swear to anything that comes out of that post office, since he gets it from his wife and she ain't reliable. Says he ain't never seen Bert Dilly so much as scratch at a letter or package. But old Joe Moon has a handful of dirt to throw. First, he tells the court about the long-distance call he made to the state postmaster's office and wound up talking for half an hour with some lady that didn't even work there and then turns toward the state postmaster in the front row and asks him why they let just anybody answer them phones. Then he tells the court how upset his wife got at Bert and how she ain't cooked him a decent meal since. And he tells us all about her big splat outside the Stokely Courthouse when they shoved her fat butt out the door.

The judge looks over at Bert, and Bert don't show any sign of wanting to address the man. So next the lawyer calls up Crete Waller—you remember I told you about him, the nosey one. The old fool waddles down the aisle and takes the oath and plops down in the hot seat, and we can all see his forehead gleaming with sweat.

"Now, Mr. Waller," the law devil says, grinning again, "just what can you tell this court about the Stokely post office?" At this point, the lawyer turns his head and faces us.

And Crete pipes up, "Well, it needs a new coat of paint inside and out, if you ask me." And there goes the gavel again for the tenth time today. And Judge Huff has to issue another stern warning to us all that he will clear the courtroom if he hears so much as a snicker. But we can't help it that Crete Waller is a little off-center—and if you ask me, I think that little lawyer almost laughed hisself.

"What I mean, Mr. Waller, is how often do you go to the post office, and have you had any mail problems?"

"Seventeen!" Crete blurts out quickly, and everybody is speechless.

"Seventeen what, Mr. Waller?" the law devil asks him.

"Seventeen times," Crete replies. "Seventeen times last month. Or do you want it by the week? You want me to figure up how many for my whole life? Cause that could take a while, and I would need a piece of paper and pencil. I don't figure so good in my head anymore. Not since I got kicked by that horse back during the war. Do you want me to do some adding?"

I tell you, that Judge Huff looks fit to be tied. He doesn't bang his hammer or yell or even wag a finger at old Crete. He just stares at the man like some strange creature he ain't never seen before. That's the best I can describe it. And even though we all know Crete's a little low on smart, this beats anything we ever saw. The lawyer man just stands there staring, too, and I think Crete would have gone right on like that, except the judge finally looks over at Bert and asks him to please stand up and make a statement on his own behalf.

"Your Honor," Bert says, "I'd be glad to do that for you, but I don't know why it's my fault Nettie Moon ain't got good balance or why Joe Moon there was so dumb he didn't even ask the woman at the state post office her name—or even if he reached the right place. And he's been telling everybody for years his wife can't cook worth a flip to begin with. And as for Crete Waller here, all he's got left is his pilot light. You can't expect him to remember too much."

You can hear a pin drop in the courtroom, and the squeaky little lawyer asks the judge for a recess till next morning, and down comes that hateful little hammer again for its last bang of the day.

Lord, am I ready to get up and leave. If I was a drinking woman, I'd find the first watering hole and crawl into a whiskey

bottle. It sure don't take long for the men to locate the closest local bar. Some of us walk down to the street to the Catfish
Corral and eat our bait of catfish and hushpuppies and discuss
the situation across the table—even though the judge said not to.
You can't shut people up on some things. What we do next is we
all split up and everybody's on their own finding sleeping accom-
modations. Some have relatives, some brought sleeping bags that
they roll out right there in the parking garage, and some ride
around looking for cheap rooms. I myself sleep on the bus the
first night. Even with the windows all down, it still smells bad
as it did when we rolled into town. And sure enough, there sets
Noleen, pouted up in the back seat waiting for us to return. Only
a few of us do—I don't take count. I just close my eyes, and when
I wake up, the mosquitoes have damn near drained the blood
from my body. I decide right then and there to get a room the
next night. I tell you, come morning I look like I went ten rounds
with a buzz saw from all the welts and scratching.

Day two of the hearing goes about like day one, only half
of us come straggling in late because nobody thought to bring
an alarm clock. Bert shows up in his blue serge suit again, and I
swear to myself I'm gonna buy that man a new suit if we ever get
him back home. He ain't bought a new stitch since Harry and
Bess Truman moved into the White House.

They already have the big ceiling fans on when we get there—
probably still airing the smell out of the place from the day
before, and it feels cool for a change. I take some pancake from
my compact and try to cover up some of the mosquito bites and
all when I see how they stick out under the bright lights, and I
settle myself back down next to the floozy again. And then all
of a sudden, we hear this commotion in the back. It seems Miss
Opal and Tallulah Bunn got stopped by a bailiff wanting to know
what Opal's carrying in her big satchel. We can all hear the two
sisters out there trying to boss the man around till he finally just
snatches it away from her and shoves them through the door.
Ain't supposed to bring nothing bigger than your purse into the

courtroom—the bailiff made that clear yesterday. So they grouse and groan their way to their seats behind me again, and I turn around and shush them soon as the bailiff calls us to our feet, and they don't like that one bit. What goes around comes around, is all I can say.

Most of the second day is cut short by recesses and some kind of emergency that drags Judge Huff away from his throne. And they still ain't got around to Faye Bawcom yet. I tell you, folks are getting so perturbed they're ready to drive her up to the witness chair with a stick. We don't understand why the sneaky little law devil didn't call her up first thing. The only two people we hear from the second day is Elmo Wissler and Miss Lottie Sweet, and you can't believe a word neither one of them says. Elmo's the town drunk and Miss Lottie don't even go to church no more. So I ask you, what's the good of having them two swear to tell the truth on the *Holy Bible*? Far as we're all concerned, it's just a day wasted, and now we got to look for sleeping arrangements again. Since I ain't really got the money to spare, I decide to sleep on the bus again. But I do go to the dime store first and invest in some air freshener to spray the place down—only now it smells like somebody threw up in a gardenia bush. I'm dead tired by the time I get settled, but I don't get a wink of sleep. You'd think the smell alone would repel the damn mosquitoes.

On the third and final day of the hearing, the crap hits the fan right off. Bert stands up pretty as you please and tells the bailiff: "Have a seat." Can you believe that? Says he's thought about how hard it must be to stand up all day long, shifting from one foot to the other, and don't the judge think so, too. I ain't got the words to describe the look of the judge's face this time. He tries to cut Bert off, but Bert just keeps right on talking: how guilty he feels making the bailiff stand up straight all day, how he's taking up all our time and money coming all this way, and how expensive it must be to pay that squeaky little lawyer with the people's taxes. And the bailiff finally has to hustle old Bert back into Judge Huff's chambers, and heaven only knows what he done to him back there—maybe slapped some sense into him. And the whole time, the judge and the lawyer man are just huddled up and whispering to each other.

As if the day ain't started off bad enough, you ain't gonna believe this, but up pops poor old Darla again, this time without even being recognized by the judge. "Speak up!" she yells. "This is a hearing, ain't it? Well, we can't hear a thing you're saying." And down comes the judge's gavel. But Darla just goes right on with her sermon. "You tell us we're all here to be heard, and you ain't called me up there to testify. I got my rights, and I want to testify."

The whole time she's yelling, the woman bailiff is trying to make her way to the middle of the row to drag her out of the courtroom again, but Darla don't wait. She tromps her way to the opposite aisle where she takes up her sermon again right where she left off. "Can't you see Bert Dilly ain't got sense enough to know he's done anything wrong. Hell, it ain't the Big House the man needs, it's the *Nuthouse*—in Cedarville! Him and every one of them Dillys—I've known them all. Ask him about his mama doing a back flip off a pier down in Gulfport." And it goes on like this until a bailiff from another courtroom sneaks in and drags her kicking and screaming out the side door. Lord, the names Darla calls that man make our ears sting, and I sure as hell can't repeat them for you. We find out later that they let her off with just a fine, and she has to spend the rest of the hearing on that pukey bus commiserating with Noleen Shaker.

I'm here to tell you, Darla Birdlace is a fine one to be naming candidates for Cedarville anyway. Did I tell you her daddy knocked her mama's teeth out with a two-by-four? Swore it was an accident, but folks said you could never believe a word that man said. Just the same, nobody ever contested it. Just watching Miss Darla might give you some idea what her mama was like—since she's just like her. And you remember I told you how she just hops herself a bus to nowhere-in-particular on a whim.

Finally, after all this time, it's my turn to take the hot seat, and let me tell you, my ass is working button holes the whole while. Right off the bat, the little lawyer asks me, "Now Miss Peep, what is your relationship with Mr. Bert Dilly?"

"Bert and I grew up together and been friends all our lives," I says to him, matter-of-factly as you please. He just bats his eyes at that and says, "Uh-huh."

"Now, has Mr. Dilly ever shown you any favoritism at the Stokely post office? Ever made any exceptions for you?" He's grinning at me now. Makes me want to reach over and knock out his two front teeth, and the image of it nearly makes me bust out laughing.

"No sir," I says to him. "The man treats everybody the same. Except them that are nasty to him." I'm eyeing the Bunn sisters when I say this part, and they show me a hateful look.

"Please tell the court what you know about Mr. Dilly tampering with the mail. Opening boxes and letters and such," he then says to me.

"I ain't never seen Bert—Mr. Dilly, that is—tamper or open anybody's mail in my life." I know I'm under oath, and I'm sweating bullets, since I *have* seen him prying and shaking and peeking. But that ain't exactly what the question is, so I stick to my answer.

"Have you ever been made aware of any mail tampering by neighbors or friends? Tampering by Mr. Dilly?" He's got me cornered here, and I don't know how to respond without getting poor old Bert into trouble. And then it hits me like a lightning bolt what to say.

"Stokely, Louisiana, is a small town," I says to the law devil. "If I scratch my butt on the front porch, everybody in town knows about it—and by the time the news makes its way from Jackson Street to Main Street, I've got the worst case of poison ivy you ever saw. And you want me to testify about what I hear? According to local gossip, I should've been prostrate with polio a half-dozen times. The Bunn sisters setting right over there forced Bert Dilly at gunpoint to open some boxes from Shreveport one day—just because they heard they contained dirty magazines.

And Mayor Purdy and his wife setting back there has bilked the town out of $10,000 over the past three years. Did you know they buried some Martians out there on Bert Dilly's land?"

"We're getting pretty far afield here, Miss Peep," the law devil says to me. "I just want facts, not hearsay."

"Please confine your responses to the facts, Miss Peep," Judge Huff pipes up, and looks at me sternly.

"Well sir, the fact is that there ain't no facts. I ain't heard a word spoke in this court that can't be contested." I stop here for a minute just to let this sink in and then continue. "You can't believe every word folks say in Stokely. Everybody in this court-room that came on the caravan knows damn good and well—excuse my language, Your Honor—that they wouldn't even be here if they hadn't been part of some gossip themselves." The whole time I'm talking, I'm picturing old Bert behind bars or out whacking weeds along the highways in his prison suit. And he ain't never looked good in stripes.

"You're dodging my questions, Miss Peep," the lawyer man says to me. "We've got letters here from several citizens in Stokely with allegations of deliberate mail tampering and improper pro-cedures." Then he backs off from me real slow and seems to study my reaction to this. I look over at Judge Huff, and I say, "Then ask me questions I can answer. Questions I can swear to under oath."

"Once again," the lawyer says to me, "are you aware of any instances of mail tampering at the Stokely post office? Don't stop to think about it, just answer yes or no."

"No!" I say—waiting for the floor to give way and drop me straight into Hell. "I cannot swear to something I don't know for sure. I'm afraid all I can give this court is what we brought with us—hearsay!" I leave it there, and the lawyer pitches a little fit about me dancing around his questions. And by now the judge is getting pretty upset with the both of us. I'm afraid he's gonna hold me and the lawyer both in contempt, and I'm just about to pee myself when there comes this loud gasp from the crowd.

Right in the middle of my testimony, I look up and—big as

you please—here comes J.T. and Hannah Dilly pushing Miss Lulu smack down the center aisle. The sight nearly knocks us all to our knees. It's the first time the four of them has been in the same room in over ten years. I tell you, we let out a gasp strong enough to inhale the judge's robe.

Judge Huff don't know what to make of it until the bailiff walks all the way up the aisle and tells him who the people are, and he just couldn't keep the man's mama and family out in the hall. And then that damn K-Billy Bingham jumps up and yells, "Howdy, Mrs. D!" and sets off a gab fest. The judge just looks at me setting there on the witness stand—like I had something to do with it—and then at the lawyer and finally over at Bert. It takes five bangs of his gavel to shut us all up and regain control of his courtroom.

"Is this all the evidence we have, Mr. Smelt," the judge asks the little law devil, "or do you have anything more convincing than the testimonies I've had to endure already?" The judge's face is beet red and ready to pop, and the law man don't say anything. "I'm afraid this court cannot rely on testimony based on small-town bickering and name-calling," Judge Huff says. "I haven't seen OR heard a shred of hard evidence—*credible* evidence—that anything more than gossip has happened in the town of Stokely. And this court cannot prosecute that. What have you to say, Mr. Smelt?"

The little law devil seems to shrivel up right before our eyes. He looks around the courtroom and tells the judge he ain't gonna call no more witnesses—not even Faye Bawcom. Or the fat little Catholic—who don't know any more than what he's been told by a bunch of gossips. And even though Aunt Flossie don't get her chance to sing Bert's praises neither, I know he's happy to see she made the long trip down here just for him.

With that, the judge announces loudly: "This case is dismissed. Amen!" He pushes hisself back, hikes up his robe, and disappears into his chambers. We find out later that the little law man was holding Miss Faye as his final witness—to nail his case shut.

We all just sit there. Stunned! It's a full five minutes till we snap to and realize the whole mess is over and Bert is set free. And oh, the way folks swarm around him you'd think they was everyone of them his best friend—everybody except the hateful Bunn sisters and the Moons. And I have to say, the ride back home don't seem nearly so bad as coming—except when Noleen starts in on the driver again to stop the bus and look for her tired old wig lying dead somewhere by the road.

Lord, ever since the trial mess hit the papers and the TV, tongues are wagging about it from Tickfaw to Shongaloo. Caused such a stir, the state postmaster says they're sending out a whole new list of laws and regulations to post offices all over the state of Louisiana. Bert don't really comprehend it, but he ended up kind of a celebrity—even Miss Hannah is speaking to him again. I don't know what it is, but something magical happens once people read about you in the paper or hear about you on the radio or TV set.

There ain't one lawful reason why they stuck Bert Dilly back in that post office, and yet there he is. The matter never did make it to court officially, after everything that happened. But you know he's guilty as sin, and the old fool just ain't got sense enough to recognize it. It's just his way.

So there you have it—the unvarnished story, the ugly truth about the whole damn lot of them. But they're all my friends and neighbors—the sorry bunch—and I won't hear a word against them. On a daily basis, nothing much ever happens in a small town like Stokely. If you're ready, though, I can take you over there and introduce you to him—Bert that is. Let's see—three o'clock. He ought to be about waist high in boxes and packages by now. The afternoon truck from Shreveport has come and gone. Ask him what all came in and you'll be there till midnight. He ain't changed a bit.